Murder at High Sea

A MUSICAL CRUISE COZY MURDER MYSTERY

KAREN MCSPADE

NEWCASTLE
MEDIA

Edited by Darci Heikkinen

Cover Design by Molly Burton of
cozycoverdesigns.com

This is a work of fiction. Names, characters, places, and incidents either are
products of the author's imagination or are used fictitiously. Any similarity to
actual events or locales or persons, living or dead, is entirely coincidental.

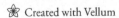 Created with Vellum

FREE GIFT

Receive your FREE exclusive copy of **Hash Browns And Homicide**, the series prequel, and get notified via email of new releases, giveaways, contests, cover reveals, and insider fun when you sign up to my VIP Mystery Book Club mailing list!

Karen McSpade

Hash Browns And Homicide

A Piper Sandstone Savory Mystery

Scan the QR Code To Sign Up and Claim Your FREE Exclusive Book

Description

*Special Note: This book is a standalone cozy mystery connected to the Piper Sandstone series which can be enjoyed on its own.

It can also be relished at anytime during the Piper Sandstone mysteries, but might be most enjoyable following the **Savory Mystery Series** or after reading the **Deep Fried Revenge Series**.

Four legendary rock stars. One killer cruise performance. Can these quirky female sleuths solve the murder mystery before their career gets axed?

A southern all-girl band from the '80s, The Delta Queens are ready to set the stage on fire aboard the Ovation with their soulful rock 'n' roll music. When their tour manager lands them the headlining show on the ship, the ladies seize the opportunity to revive their musical career and grab one last shot at fame and fortune. But there's one thing standing in the way of their success... murder at high sea.

After a rehearsal session goes awry and a member of the crew is murdered, Doris, Rosemary, Margie, and Patty Sue are caught in the spotlight of possible suspects without an alibi. To make matters worse, the ship's captain has an unconventional idea about how to best deal with the situation. The ladies don't want to follow her heartless plan, but if they cross hairs with the captain one more time, it could cost them their careers... or get them thrown overboard.

Contents

Seasick

ROSEMARY

The Delta Queens' Lead Singer

"Okay, ladies! Let's run through it again! From the top!" Carl called out. Patty Sue and I groaned in unison. Margie slumped her head on the keyboard, the keys making a funny plonking sound.

"I think that's enough for now," Ian, our tour manager, said from below the stage. "They've been rehearsing for five hours," he reminded Carl, the lines of tension visible on his forehead.

Thank goodness for our manager, dear sweet Ian. I wanted to jump off the stage and squish him in a hug. He stood there, stoic and stern, in a leather bomber jacket with his aviator shades hanging from his shirt. He had watched *Top Gun* too many times to count and thought we wouldn't notice when he dyed his hair dark to resemble Tom Cruise.

I recalled when we had first hired him as our manager, after deciding to take The Delta Queens beyond our home state of

1

Alabama. Doris, Patty Sue, Margie, and I enjoyed a remarkable musical career, rising to the top as an all-female rock band in the mid-1970s. Our popularity skyrocketed, and by the early eighties, we were filling stadiums and arenas as the headline act. Ian had been there for us the entire time. Even during the rough patches. Now, as middle-aged singers trying to make a comeback in 1989, Ian came through for us again - the opportunity as the headline show on the Ovation was just what we needed to revive our careers. We owed him a lot.

"*I'm* the technical director on this ship, buddy," Carl snapped at Ian, bringing me back to the present and our seemingly endless rehearsal. Even from backstage, his voice reverberated through the empty performance hall. "I'm in charge, and I call the shots."

What a thumpin' gizzard. He'd better be thankful he looked a lot like Van Halen's previous lead singer, David Lee Roth, or I woulda' smacked him right in the kisser.

Or maybe not. I wouldn't wanna ruin that beautifully sculpted jaw. Maybe just a little whack upside the head. Still, no amount of handsome should go around bossing us like that.

"We could do this in our sleep, buddy," I snapped back. "Do you really want to wear out the talent the night before their big show? It's way past midnight, and we need our beauty sleep."

"I second that. I think my hand is gonna fly right off my wrist," said Patty Sue. She removed the bass guitar strapped to her chest, a gorgeous classic Fender she'd had for decades.

"C'mon, y'all. One more round can't hurt. Tomorrow's the big sold-out show. So let's end the eighties on a high note!" Doris said, shaking out her bright red hair and beaming like the

Energizer bunny from behind her drum set. She had been trying to get us all excited, but the rest of us were just plain exhausted.

"Well, I need a break. All this sloshing around is making me seasick." It was my first time on a cruise ship, and after two days, I still had not found my "sea legs," or whatever they called it. My stomach had been churning like a cement mixer on steroids. Not fun.

"Oh, please, Rosemary. It's not that bad," said Carl. His golden hair was pulled into a ponytail tonight. His hands were on his hips, and he looked like a Greek god in his tight-fitting royal blue t-shirt that brought out his stunning eyes. *He must work out a lot. He probably smells fresh and clean, like the ocean too.*

"Speak for yourself. I'd rather not puke on stage, thank you very much," I said. It didn't help that the music hall onboard the Ovation was stinking huge, with a stage in the middle and a lower second floor filled with chairs and tables. All this open space was making me even dizzier.

"Trust me. You wouldn't want to see that." Patty Sue shuddered at the thought.

"Fine, whatever. Let's take five," huffed Carl, rolling those pretty blue eyes at me. He probably always got away with being an absolute jerk because he was so handsome.

"Oh, thank goodness. I was really craving a little water break," chirped Margie as we all scampered down the stage for a drink of water.

Onstage, the spotlights felt like giant white suns reducing us to a puddle. There were at least twenty bright lights right above us, all connected by intricate beams and cables that extended all the way backstage.

"Hi there," came a woman's high-pitched voice from behind us, making us all jump.

"Oh, jeepers! Where did you come from?" At this late hour, I was pretty sure the music hall was empty save for us, Ian, Carl, and the sound guy, Rick. Why would guests on the cruise ship be roaming around here this late?

The woman was smiling at us, her white teeth gleaming and a pair of bright green eyes hiding behind thick-rimmed glasses. Her hair was teased up to the heavens. Under her blazer, it looked like her shoulder pads had their own shoulder pads. She looked young, somewhere in her mid-twenties. "I'm Monica. Monica Hill from *Rockstar Magazine*."

"Hello, Monica Hill from *Rockstar Magazine*," I said with a little smirk. "I'm Rosemary, and this is—"

"Doris, Margie, and Patty Sue," she finished for me. "I'm such a big fan. I've seen you guys on tour! In Alabama, Florida, and Tennessee... you guys are just incredible! I so, so love your old songs! 'Feel the Beat' and 'Crazy of Us.' Those are the best!" She spoke like she had just downed a couple of espresso shots.

"No love for our new songs, hm?" I lifted a stern eyebrow and watched her cheeks turn a light shade of pink.

"Oh no! Not at all! I love all your stuff! I just meant...."

"Relax, kiddo. I'm just messin' with ya."

"*Rockstar Magazine*?" Doris asked, scrunching her forehead. "I don't think I've heard of it before."

"Oh, it's a small publication based in Houston. I mostly write fluff pieces. Small events and concerts, stuff like that. My real passion is true crime mysteries and thrillers," she said, excitement bubbling in her voice. Then her eyes widened when she realized what she had said.

"Not that you guys are... are fluff or small or anything!

4

That's not what I meant at all!" she backtracked as she fiddled with her glasses.

"That's quite alright." Margie cleared her throat. "What can we help you with?"

"I was hoping I could write a piece about you guys. I'd sort of follow you around as you do your groundbreaking cruise ship tour here on The Ovation."

Groundbreaking for an aging rock band, I guess. I knew I shouldn't have read all that bull written in the tabloids. But I just couldn't help it. Curiosity killed the cat and all that.

Delta Queens Running Out Of Gigs? was what one of the papers had printed, and in annoying big black print too. *Four-piece rock band books a cruise ship tour on The Ovation after their last three albums are critically and commercially panned. Is this the end for the once-famed rock legends?*

"I mean, you're The Delta Queens," Monica kept going. "You guys are legendary!"

Legendary? More like historic. As in, we're ancient history, perhaps?

"I want the readers to feel like they're here on the ship with you guys," she continued. "I'm going to write the whole deal. Behind the scenes, backstage stuff. All of it."

"Well, that sounds lovely," Margie said amicably, and we nodded along with her.

I turned my back to Monica and whispered, "What do you think, girls? This is our big chance to revive our music career, and some good press could be the boost we need."

"Well, it can't hurt. We still haven't recovered from that incident in Nashville," Doris reminded us, her eyebrows raised.

"That was the stupid media's fault!" I used both free arms to make air quotes as I recited the headline that nearly sabotaged our musical career. "The Delta Queens' encore ends in drunken disaster." I felt my face flush and my temperature rise as I remembered the lies the media spun for a trending headline.

"You're right, Rose. It wasn't nice of them to write those things about you. It was a legitimate costume malfunction, and you converted that scarf to a halter top in the blink of an eye," Margie soothed, rubbing my back.

"Honestly though, darlin', how was the media supposed to know it was a sudden attack of vertigo and not a drunken stupor that landed you in the front row of the audience?" Patty Sue added.

"Well, if they had bothered to interview us, we could have cleared it all up," I hissed before Doris peeked over at Monica and then back to us.

"Ladies, we can't change the past, so let's not waste time worrying over it. Monica is offering us some positive press. We would be crazy to turn her down." Doris smiled as she put her arms around our necks.

"Especially since Ian had to bend over backward to get this gig for us. Thank goodness Hall and Oates and Air Supply were double booked, but talk about pressure."

"Let's go, ladies! Your five minutes are up!" called Carl, materializing from somewhere backstage.

"Here we go again," huffed Patty Sue before taking one last gulp of water.

"Oh, I'm so sorry for taking up your time. I'll get out of your way and let you guys rehearse. Just let me know what you decide," Monica said. "And break a leg!"

Suddenly, the door to the music hall swung open, and a staff member handed Ian a small piece of paper before dashing off.

"Geesh, someone sure knows how to crack the whip around here," I whispered to Ian, nodding my head toward Carl as we made our way back onstage.

"Hmm? Oh... um... yeah. Cracking the whip. Ha," he said without looking at me. He read the message and then started wadding the flimsy piece of paper up in his hands.

"You alright?"

"Yeah. Yes. Fine. I... uhh... just got a message." His hand went up to his chin, rubbing at his stubble. "There's someone I need to call back right away. You guys go on ahead and practice. I'll be right back."

He walked quickly to the exit and was out the door before I could say anything else.

"Where's he running off to, Rose?" Margie asked me.

"Says he had to make a call."

"C'mon, c'mon! I haven't got all day," Carl yelled again, clapping his hands together like a boot camp officer rounding up a bunch of lagging privates." A shrill ringing sound from the phone backstage interrupted his tirade. He promptly ignored it and scowled at us from the stage since we weren't moving fast enough.

"Rick!" he snapped at the sound guy checking our instruments. "I thought I told you to plug the DI box into the mixing console. Are you deaf or just dumb?"

"But you told me not to—"

"The synths sound like we're stuck in the belly of a whale. The harmonics are flat as a pancake. And I told you to lock the door backstage. And answer that damn phone while you're back there. Do I have to tell you everything?"

Poor, sweet Rick. He'd been in Carl's crosshairs all night. But that's how Carl treated all the tech crew members doing the grunt work. It was despicable. We'd only been here two days, and we'd already seen enough.

"Got it, boss. I'll get on it right away." Rick still managed to smile, showing off his cute dimples before walking behind the velvet curtains to do Carl's bidding. The patience he had was astounding.

I heard the clang and clatter of the door being locked backstage. "Who the heck does this guy think he is?" I whispered to the rest of the group. "The Queen of England?"

"He's obviously too big for his britches, as my mama used to say," Doris admitted. "But this is still a job. I know we're all exhausted. Let's not mind him and just focus on our music."

"Good point, Doris." I took a deep breath. "Let's focus on the music. That's easy. I can do that."

I took my position in front of the stage, gripping the microphone tightly as I waited for the opening notes of Doris's drums to "Is This the End." It was one of our newer songs, a crooning ballad with an upbeat rock tempo.

Margie's keyboard provided the rich, sweet melody as I started the first line. "Goodbye is said and done." I strummed the opening chords on my electric guitar, the strap burning on my neck.

Then I heard Patty Sue's voice, soft, low, and clear alongside mine. "Searching for something better. All awake look for land. For every man's in a hurry."

Doris and I wrote the lyrics for this song years ago. Patty Sue and Margie came up with the melody. Strangely, it was right after the release of our third album, and we read all that horrible trash in the reviews. I remember clutching that flimsy newspaper so hard that the black ink bled onto my hand. We promised ourselves we wouldn't think about it. What does *The*

New York Review know about good music anyway? And within a few hours, we came up with a new song that hit the charts.

"Can we just slow it down tonight? Can we just pick back up the faith?" The music swelled, a cascade of emotions from the very depths of my soul. The crescendo of tones filled the hall, reaching beyond the rafters. From the corner of my eye, I could see Monica in the wings of the stage, looking at us in complete awe.

We were a single voice, an orchestra in perfect harmony. The melody was intense as I belted out the chorus. It was slow, rolling and crashing like a big wave. "Can we just sit for a moment? Can we just slow it down tonight?"

My voice rose high, following the sweet, piping notes of Margie's keyboard. The pounding of the drums thrummed in unison. "What else could you be looking for? To live is to find yourself. Too powerful for love."

Higher and higher my voice went, following the raspy belt of Patty Sue's singing. I was flying; our music soared past the steel walls and deep black water beneath us. "Too powerful for love...."

One moment, there was my voice, heavenly and raw, transcending time and space. And then, out of nowhere—

BAM!!!

A loud crash, ugly and deafening. Behind me, all I heard was glass smashing and metal clanking, drowning out our music. It echoed and cracked like a storm on the warpath. And then, an even louder thud. My singing turned into a screech, an otherworldly sound so different from mere seconds ago.

"What in the name of Zeus was that?"

"Are you guys okay? Everyone okay?" Doris asked. She was

crouching behind her drum set, eyes flitting back and forth between the rest of us.

"I... I think so. My heart leaped out of my ribcage there," Margie mumbled, clutching her hand to her chest.

A hushed silence descended on us as we tried to figure out what had happened. "It... it came from backstage," Monica said, her voice unsteady.

"What in the world happened?" Rick came rushing from the side of the stage and joined us on the apron. He stared at us, his brow scrunched in confusion, and then he pulled back the velvet curtain with the slow carefulness of a doctor performing surgery.

That's when we saw it, the mangled beam of metal surrounded by a sea of broken glass, shimmering under the fallen stage lights. Underneath it all was a body wearing a tight blue t-shirt. A golden ponytail. A perfectly sculpted face covered in blood.

"Oh no!" The gasps came out of our mouths in unison.

"It's... it's Carl," I squeaked.

Margie reached for my hand, all the blood draining from her face. "Oh, my! This can't be happening!"

Tidal Wave

PATTY SUE

Bass Guitarist

"This is bad... really, really bad." Margie looked about, ready to hyperventilate. Or pass out. Whichever might come first. "What do we do? What do we do?"

"Okay, let's not panic," Doris said, her voice shaky in a way I had never heard before. If anything, that made Margie panic even more.

I looked at the lighting equipment. "It looks like the entire panel of stage lights fell and clocked Carl before he could escape."

"Those lights look heavy too. Each one is like a giant bowling ball with an LED light attached at the end. Twenty pounds or so, I would guess," Doris calculated.

"The poor thing. Carl looks like he could just be asleep if not for the blood and whatnot," Margie winced. "Right on his head, the huge thing fell."

"How on Earth could that light panel just plunge down from its perch all the way up there?" Doris stared up into the rafters, deep in thought.

"I... I think I'm gonna throw up," I heard Monica mutter.

"Do we... um... do CPR or something? Mouth to mouth resuscitation?" Rosemary said with a slight grimace. When we all turned to her with an incredulous look, she just shrugged and went, "What? I'm not a paramedic."

"I'll call for help," Rick offered as he bounded for the exits. He took off so fast that I wondered if he was going for help or running away.

"Yep. Uh-huh. I'm definitely gonna throw up," Monica said. "I'm... I'm gonna... need a bucket." She stumbled around further backstage, and a few seconds later, we heard her retching and groaning into a pail.

The girls and I shifted our focus from Carl to Monica, to the door that Rick had dashed through, and back to Carl's body again in utter shock before Doris broke the silence.

"Oh, Jiminy Cricket. This isn't happening. This can't be happening," Doris cried, clutching at her hair. All vestiges of calm crashed down when she started pacing back and forth. "Not on our last-chance tour!"

I whipped my head toward her so fast that I think my neck cricked a little. "Doris! The guy is dead!"

"Exactly! Think of the headlines! They'll write more vile things about us, I'm sure. Next thing you know, we'll be performing at subway stations and asking for change!" Doris was angry whispering now, probably for the sake of the journalist we had with us at the moment. That didn't matter, really, because Monica was still occupied with her bucket.

"Now, now. Let's not... jump to conclusions," Margie said

with a hint of bravery in her tone, though the blood hadn't quite returned to her face yet. "He might... still be alive," she quietly offered, her eyes still glued to Carl's body.

We stared at him some more; no one moved an inch. The poor thing. And he was such a young guy too. Probably not past his late thirties... about our age.

"Let me just...." Margie moved gingerly toward Carl, side-stepping the cables coiled next to him. She placed two fingers on the side of his neck, trying to feel a pulse. I could tell by the look on her face that she felt nothing.

"He's... gone."

"Oh, this is not good. What if we get blamed for this?" Doris started to fidget, shuffling her feet around. "I think it would be best if we weren't involved with this at all. What if... what if we leave now and just let the staff members deal with it? I mean, since we don't even know what happened to him."

"That's a terrible idea. That would make us look even more suspicious!" I gestured to Monica, who was still recovering, slumped away in a corner backstage. "Plus, we've got Pukey McPukerson over there. She already knows we're here."

"It was an accident, Doris. Accidents happen all the time." Margie's voice was soft like a soothing balm.

Doris sighed. "We can't have any more bad publicity. We need this tour. Okay, I need this tour. If we end up in jail, our music career is over, and I don't have—"

"Look, I know you have a lot riding on this...." I sighed, knowing that Doris was going through a hard time. With her husband, Bill, losing his job and her young daughter in an expensive private school, money was tight. To make matters worse, she had told us that Bill was leaving her for another woman, one of his students. The dirty, lying cheat! And now this. Doris did not need to be suspected of foul play right now.

Doris walked back to her drum set and flopped down on the stool. She looked so tired and much older all of a sudden. "A lot? Yeah, that's an understatement, Patty."

I reached over and touched her shoulder to console her when the door swung open and heavy footsteps filled the hall. Doris sighed again and threw her hands in the air. "Oh, sweet heavens, here we go. That's probably the cops."

"Relax. Maybe it's just Rick with the medics or something."

Ian came into view and walked quickly toward the stage. "Hey, girls. Are you... uh... what happened?"

No one answered. With all four of us crowded around the stage, it somehow hid the view of Carl's body but not the mangled metal beams.

"Is everyone okay?" He jumped up on stage, the glass crunching under his shoes. "What—oh!"

"So..." Rosemary started like she was talking about the weather. "There was an accident."

"An accident?" Ian looked away, clenching and unclenching his hands. "What in the world happened?"

"This whole beam fell, and one of the spotlights hit Carl in the head." I looked at the tangle of cables that were supposed to support the beam. Both ends had a thick, rope-like cable still attached to them. However, as I traced the length of the cables, I noticed one side had frayed, broken wires that had snapped right through. "Hmm... this is interesting."

"What?" came Monica's voice from behind us.

The ladies and Ian turned to me as Monica joined us from behind the velvet curtain, still looking a little green.

"Look here. The cable attached to this side of the beam is

frayed." Sure enough, the twisted metal twine looked worn out and tattered. "That doesn't look very safe. That's probably what caused the crash."

"The equipment here might be old and not well-maintained," suggested Margie. "Like I said, it was an unfortunate accident. Right, Patty?"

"I suppose so." Still, there was something off about those cables. I wouldn't think a thick metal cable could just fray like that on its own.

Ian let out a breath he didn't seem to know he was holding. "Hoo boy. This is a mess."

Doris whipped her head at him. "Is it bad? What do you think's gonna happen? Will the show be canceled?"

"I... I don't know," he said. He kept rubbing at his stubble. We'd known Ian for a long time, and this was a sure sign of distress. After all, he had to pull a lot of strings for us to get this gig. We might be "legendary rockstars" and whatnot, but there were other music groups that were way more popular than us. Blondie. The Go-Go's. Pat Benatar. All of them were cooler, trendier, and much bigger than our little girl band from Alabama. They could bring in bigger crowds and, in turn, more money.

"Wait, did someone call for help?" Ian asked. "I mean, I don't think we should just be standing around over a dead body."

"Rick went outside to call for help."

"Right. Okay, good." He rubbed his stubble again. In his other hand, I noticed a small ball of paper crumpled in his fist. "Well, I guess there's nothing else we can do but wait for the medical staff to arrive."

Dead in the Water

DORIS

The Drumming Queen

"Lemme get this straight. It just fell?" Captain Doherty asked in a thick New Yorker accent that made it sound like she was speaking directly through her nose. She was still in her crisp white uniform, with the starchy cap and epaulets. Everything about her seemed to be put together with military precision, from the bobby pins keeping her brown hair secured tightly to the immaculate shine of her shoes. Her eyes, however, were wild and intense as she surveyed the stage.

Of all the people Rick could have found, of course, it had to be the captain of the entire stinking ship. Why couldn't it have been someone with a less intimidating uniform? There was no chance of us getting out of this now. A groan started to bubble up in my stomach. Maybe I was going to be sick too.

"The cables holding up this side of the beam are frayed,"

Patty Sue said, pointing to the offending wires. "That might have caused it."

The captain sighed and pinched her nose, looking quite queasy herself. Murder on a cruise ship. Her cruise ship. That was going to cause some waves and not the kind anyone wanted to ride in the calm Caribbean waters where the ship was headed. Guess we weren't the only ones who didn't need the bad press.

"What do we do?" came Margie's faint voice.

Her gaze didn't break from Carl's body, her look a thousand miles away. "We'll have to contact the family."

"He doesn't have family," Rick piped in.

"No?"

"He was an orphan. He got drunk one time and told us all about it."

When we all gave him a questioning look, he just shrugged. "We've worked together on a few different cruise ships."

"So, no wife? Kids?"

Rick shook his head.

"Girlfriend, at least?"

There was a beat of silence before Rick answered again. "No. No girlfriend."

Captain Doherty crouched down near Carl's body to study him, so close I worried the blood would somehow get on her pristine white uniform. "Hm. A lone wolf. Interesting."

"Guess he doesn't have a lot of friends either," I heard Rosemary mutter under her breath. Margie nudged her in the ribs.

"Technically, that would be true," said Rick. "He doesn't really stay in one place for too long. Jumps from one gig to another, one cruise ship to another. This one time, he just up and left for the Bahamas."

Captain Doherty started nodding. I could see the gears turning in her brain. "Okay, okay. Good. That's good."

"How is that good?" Rosemary asked.

"Look, we'll cooperate with the authorities, give our statements," Ian interjected. "Whatever we need to do, we'll do it."

So much for us getting out of this whole mess. "Are we in any trouble? I mean... will our shows be canceled?

The captain didn't respond; she just kept staring at Carl. Her crouched figure cast a long shadow across the stage.

I felt the ship sway slightly, just enough to rattle the doors of the venue. I craned my neck to peer outside. I tried to imagine the darkness beyond the doors, the sloshing of the waves as they lapped up on the sides of the ship. Here, wrapped in the twinkling colorful lights of the music hall, it felt like we were in some weird bubble.

"Who else knows?" the captain asked.

Ian scrunched up his face like he always did when he was confused. "What do you mean?"

"Who else was here? Who else knows that he's dead?"

"Just... us. We were the only ones here," I admitted.

The captain stood up and wiped her hands on her trousers. Then she shook her head like she had just made up her mind. "No."

"No?" I parroted.

"We're not calling the cops," the captain said.

"I'm... I'm sorry. I don't understand," said Margie.

"Well, there's not much to understand. We are going to keep this whole thing quiet."

Did I hear her right, or was my tortured mind now playing tricks on me?

"But why?" asked Rosemary.

The captain took off her cap and wiped the sweat off her brow. "Look, the last thing my guests need ruining their fun vacation is a dead body on the ship."

"But... there *is* a dead body on the ship. He's right stinkin' there!" Rosemary pointed at Carl.

Captain Doherty smiled at Rosemary, the kind of smile that didn't really feel like one. Like Mona Lisa's. "They don't need to know that, do they?"

"That's crazy. He's the technical director of this show. The crew members will ask about him," said Rick.

"This is for everyone's well-being," she continued. "We can't have guests panicking and freaking out, do you understand?" The captain tapped her immaculate shoes. "You said it yourself. Carl was a bit of a wild stallion, wasn't he?"

"Well, yes. But—"

"Is there an assistant technical director?" she interrupted.

Rick looked taken aback. "That would be Jeffrey."

"Can he do the job?"

"Umm... yes, I think so," Rick stammered.

The captain put her cap back on. "Good. Tell them Carl is... out with the flu. Then when we reach the next port, tell them Carl took a flight out to... Colorado. He got tired of the sun and wanted to head for the mountains."

Rick ran his hands through his buzzcut. His shirt was drenched in sweat. "I... I can't just... say something like that. W-what about the body then, huh?"

"Well, we do have a morgue onboard. We'll keep him there until we reach the next port in Barbados. I have connections with the police there. They can handle it."

"This is absurd! I'm calling the cops!" Monica said, looking less green now and more red with anger.

The captain shrugged. "What cops? We're in international waters."

"The Coast Guard then!"

"Again, they have no jurisdiction here."

"I'm not going to just stand here and do nothing!" Monica spat.

Captain Doherty's face didn't flinch. "Unless you can bring a dead man back to life, save your breath. The faster we can sweep this under the rug, the better it'll be for all of us."

Monica's eyes burned with rage. "What kind of captain are you?"

"The kind who's thinking of the common good. This was an unfortunate accident, one our guests don't need to concern themselves with."

Monica scoffed. "I'm sorry for throwing a wrench in your nice, little plan, but I'm a journalist. As soon as we reach port, I'll—"

"Really?" Captain Doherty's face finally broke a little, looking surprised and genuinely impressed. "For a newspaper?"

"Umm... no," Monica backtracked, her face suddenly shy. "It's a... a magazine."

"Which magazine exactly?"

"It's called... *Rockstar Magazine*."

"*Rockstar Magazine*? Never heard of it."

Monica sighed. "It's a small, up-and-coming publication based in Houston."

The corners of the captain's mouth moved a few inches upward, looking pleased and predatory. When she didn't say anything else, Monica started babbling to fill up the tense silence.

"I'm working on my portfolio so that I can move up to a

bigger, more well-known magazine. It's... it's just a temporary thing, you know," Monica said, all the bite gone out of her voice.

"My brother works in publication," Captain Doherty started. "Norman Doherty. You've probably heard of him."

Monica's eyes nearly bugged out of her skull. "Wait, *the* Norman Doherty? The editor-in-chief of *Crime Watch*?"

The captain smiled again. "Exactly. So, you can imagine the contacts he has."

We watched their conversation unfold like a particularly intense tennis match. Where was the captain going with this exactly?

"Wh-what are you saying?" Monica stuttered.

The captain hummed, then tapped her shoe. One bobby pin in her hair had started sliding out of place. "If this gets out, I will make sure you'll be stuck at your small-town magazine for the rest of your career."

"What?" we cried in unison. Our voices echoed around the stage.

"You can't be serious," Monica said, turning pale again.

Captain Doherty steeled her face. "I'm the captain here. It's my job to do what's best for the entire ship."

"And you think that means blackmailing the poor girl?" Ian was shouting now, but the captain just stared at him blankly.

"If that's what I have to do, then yes." Captain Doherty turned toward us and added, "And I'll also make sure you won't get any work on a cruise line ever again."

"This is crazy. You're out of your mind, lady," Rosemary scoffed at her. Even with her confidence, her voice wobbled a little.

"Oh, I'm sorry. I forgot you got a whole bunch of gigs just

lined up and waitin' for ya," the captain snapped back, voice dripping with sarcasm. "I don't know why you're making such a big deal about this. If this mess gets out, this is bad for your career too."

I watched Ian's throat bob up and down. He was rubbing at his stubble again. The girls all looked at me, our eyes having a private conversation.

What do we do? Margie's eyes were pinging around as if the answer to our dilemma was written on one of the walls.

This lady is off her rocker. Is her plan seriously going to work? Rosemary looked annoyed, her eyes darting from us to Ian.

It doesn't look like we have a choice. I shook my head, defeated. They understood and nodded in sync.

"And the same goes for you," Captain Doherty said pointedly at Rick. "You'll be out on the streets looking for another job before you can even sneeze."

Rick put his head down and raised his hands like he was surrendering. "I... I don't want any trouble, alright? I need this job. I... I have a family back home."

"Then you know what you need to do, don't you?"

Rick sighed. He was still sweating like a faucet. His grey shirt was nearly black.

"I'll transport the body to the morgue and get this cleaned up."

"Great!" Captain Doherty clapped her hands, looking pleased as punch. "Looks like we all have a deal here, ladies and gentlemen."

It looked like it wasn't just me who had a lot riding on this cruise ship. And I wasn't quite sure how to feel about all of this.

Smells Fishy

MARGIE

Playing the Keyboard

"Well, that was totally weird. Did we really just make a deal with the she-devil?" Rosemary said in awe and disbelief.

"It's not like she gave us much choice," Doris said. We were all squeezed together on our sofa. Ian was pacing around our cabin.

He managed to snag us a two-bedroom suite on the upper deck while he had a single room next door. The room wasn't as fancy as a Las Vegas high-roller's suite, but it had a pair of small bedrooms with two twin beds in each. There was a large bathroom we all shared and a small living area with a sofa and a chair that was now buried under a pile of potential outfits for our upcoming performance—if it still happened.

At least we had a few round windows perched right on the opposite side of the couch. Most of the passenger cabins didn't have that. We could sit around and watch the ocean go by.

Although right now, with the full moon covered by the clouds, it was ink-black darkness out there.

"Maybe she'll come around and change her mind." The words came out of my mouth on autopilot. Surely, Captain Doherty wasn't all that bad. She was a captain, after all, and she was responsible for looking out for everyone on the ship.

"Didn't you hear her, Margie? She's going to ruin all our careers and make our lives a living H-E-double-hockey-sticks," Patty Sue replied.

"Maybe if we talked to her... we could convince her to do the right thing," I offered.

Patty Sue shook her head. "She seemed pretty dead set on not letting the authorities know. And when Rick said that Carl didn't have any family, it's like she was almost... ecstatic."

"Exactly! That was such a weird reaction," Rosemary said.

Doris picked up a magazine lying on the coffee table and started flipping through it. "No point dwelling on it. It was an accident."

Rosemary shook her head, her blonde waves flopping around her head. "Don't tell me you agree with her."

"I don't agree with her necessarily. I just think she has a point. The authorities will handle it when we arrive at the next port."

"I really don't understand why we have to hide it. Like he was... murdered or something," I shuddered.

"Look, nobody wanted this to happen, Margie," Doris said, eyes still firmly planted on the magazine. "If we reported the accident to the cops, what good would that do? He's already gone."

Patty Sue's head perked up. "Are we sure that nobody wanted it to happen?"

That was an interesting thought. Unnerving but interesting. "What do you mean?" I urged.

"Margie, the whole beam fell right when he was standing there!" she exclaimed. "Don't you think it's a little bit fishy?"

Doris shrugged, still going through her magazine and flipping pages at random. "It could just be an unfortunate coincidence. Right place at the wrong time kinda thing."

"Or it could be something else," Patty Sue insisted.

Doris finally looked up, a peculiar expression painting her face. "What are you thinking?

"Are you suggesting he was murdered?" I gasped.

I could see the gears turning in Patty Sue's head. "I don't know yet. There's not a lot to go on, just that those cables broke and brought the whole beam down."

"You don't think someone... cut those cables, do you?" I whispered. The thought gave me goosebumps. That would be just ridiculous, wouldn't it? Completely impossible. Right? Who would even want to do that?

Patty Sue shrugged. "Well, there's no way to know for sure."

"Why would someone even want to kill him? I mean, sure, he's an insufferable hunk of a man, but murder?" said Rosemary.

It was quiet before I heard Doris murmur. "Maybe there's more to Carl than meets the eye."

Patty Sue leaned forward with a look that said she meant business. "Okay, so let's get this straight: we started our set, and he ducked off backstage like he usually does when we practice."

She was right. We had practiced for a few hours the day before, and I had noticed he never stood in front of the stage while we performed. He was always running around backstage and barking orders at the tech crew.

"Our song barely finishes when the beam crashes and the heavy stage light hits him in the head," Patty Sue continued, her voice rising in pitch like we were all gathered around a campfire, and she was telling a ghost story.

"There were only six of us there at the time of the crash. Us four, Monica, and Rick," Rosemary added.

"The captain was so intent on keeping this whole thing a secret. Do you think she had something to do with this?" Patty Sue asked.

"I don't see how. She wasn't there in the music hall with us. And why would she even do that? What would she have to gain?" Doris inquired, her tone still calm.

"Beats me. Maybe she ordered someone to do it for her," I suggested.

Doris sighed and closed her magazine. "Y'all, are we really turning this into a murder investigation?"

Patty Sue raised her hand in mock surrender. "We're not investigating. Let's just call it... curiosity."

Doris's green eyes turned into sharp daggers. "That's the thing that killed the cat, wasn't it?"

"Wait! Ian! You went outside right before we started, remember?" Rosemary exclaimed. All our heads turned toward our manager. Ian finally stopped his pacing and stuffed his hands in his pockets. "Hmm? Oh, yes. I... I had to make a call. I used the phone from the staff quarters."

"Did you see anyone come in or out of the music hall? Notice anyone suspicious at all?"

"Erm... no. No one suspicious. I didn't notice anyone. There was no one around," Ian stammered, choking out the words quickly before he took another breath.

"Really? You were gone for quite a while."

He rubbed at his chin and started pacing again. "I was in the staff quarters, so I didn't... I couldn't see anyone come in or out... of the music hall. I didn't see anybody."

"Oh." Rosemary looked disappointed. "Well, alright then."

"What do you think of all this? Does it seem like an accident to you?" Patty Sue asked.

"Could be. You know... who's to say?" Ian answered with a vague shrug. It was only then that I noticed he avoided looking us in the eyes.

"Should we follow the captain's orders and just leave it alone?" Patty Sue pressed on. She was an unstoppable force when she really set her mind to something. Yet Ian was unusually quiet. In those times when we didn't know what to do, he was usually our voice of reason.

"I... I don't know. I really don't know. Probably b-best we can do," Ian stuttered before making a beeline for the door. "I have... um... some paperwork to do in my room. So, I'll just...."

The door slammed close, and we heard his footsteps retreating down the hallway. And then he was gone.

"What in the world was that about?" Rosemary said. "He's been acting so weird lately."

"Everything about this cruise ship tour has been weird so far," Doris said with a sigh. She flopped her magazine back down on the table. I'm guessing she had not read a single word. "Maybe we're really not supposed to be here."

"Or maybe we were put here for a reason," Patty Sue quipped, trying to keep the conversation going.

"Which is what? To investigate a murder that's maybe not a murder?" Doris threw back.

It was quiet again except for the whirring of the fan in our room. When I spoke, I worried my voice wouldn't be heard. "How about we're here for our music? And for our fans?"

Outside the tiny round window, I could see the sky turning a shade of dark purple as the sun prepared to rise. "Tomorrow's our big show."

"Technically, it's today, Margie," Doris said, looking at her watch. "And it's almost sunrise, and we haven't had a wink of sleep."

Exhaustion washed over my bones like a heated blanket begging me to surrender to its warmth. The adrenaline of Carl's maybe-murder was starting to wear off, and all I wanted to do was collapse in my bed.

"Look, we can't control all the craziness going on out there, but on stage, it's just us and the music," I said.

"Margie's right," said Patty Sue. "Hard as it may be, we have to focus on our music."

Doris slowly rose to her feet and held her hands out for us to grab. "Agreed. Now, let's try to get some sleep. No matter how restless it might be."

Stage on Fire!

ROSEMARY

"Think happy thoughts. Happy thoughts. I'm not going to puke, no siree." I was chanting out loud as if my life depended on it. My tummy was flip-flopping around something awful. I was afraid if I moved around, the contents of my stomach would move around too. And if I stayed in place, the constant sloshing of the ship would get to me. I just couldn't win.

It probably didn't help that I had only gotten a few hours of sleep. I shared a room with Patty Sue, and with the way she kept tossing and turning, I'm guessing she wasn't faring any better than me. Who could possibly sleep when the image of a bloodied Carl was imprinted on our skulls?

And maybe I shouldn't have scoffed all that sushi for lunch.

"Stop saying puke!" Margie groaned. "You're gonna make me want to hurl! Oh, I knew I shouldn't have had that extra order of pasta."

"I think I forgot all the lyrics," Patty Sue mumbled, looking out at the horizon and cradling her bass guitar in her arms. Guess I wasn't the only one with a bad case of the jitters.

"I think I forgot how to play the drums," went Doris. She

looked at her drumsticks like it was the first time she'd ever seen them in her entire life.

Backstage, everything was chaos. Dozens of tech crew members were running around and yelling at each other, panicking like the queen of England was coming to visit. There were guys laying out cables and checking the soundboards.

There was another crew member lifting up a big, heavy amp like it was nothing more than a small sack of potatoes. *That guy is built like a tank. If I weren't just about to give the performance of my lifetime, I'd love to give those sore, muscular shoulders a good massage.*

The familiar smell of makeup on my face and the sound of a blow dryer whirring shook me out of my crazy thoughts. The light bulbs bordering the mirrors made the dressing room way too hot. I stared at my reflection to distract my mind from my stomach. My thick blonde hair was already feathered and layered to perfection. "Is my hair okay? Fluffy enough? Should I get another blowout? Add more hair spray?"

I was in a jumpsuit that looked like it belonged to Elvis. It was a purple ombre with gold studs running down the arms and chest. Looking in the mirror, I felt like I was glittering. I saw the rockstar I'd always been staring back at me. My nerves seemed to suddenly calm.

I was so, so ready. For the show, for the crowds, for everything. I wasn't thinking of my stomach, and I wasn't thinking of Carl. No siree.

"Where the hell is Carl? We need him to approve the setlist," barked someone outside the dressing room. Then he poked his head inside and looked around as if Carl was hiding among our rack of clothes in the corner. "Anyone seen Carl?"

The girls and I looked at each other, all rigid as stone.

"He was with you all last night, right? When you were practicing?" the guy asked again. He stepped into the room brandishing a clipboard. I had seen him around, but I didn't know his name. He had a bald head and a rather bushy mustache.

Here we go. Aaaaand I'm sweating. It was suddenly so stuffy in here. Hotter than the devil's armpits.

"Yes! Yes, he was with us!" I said with a little more enthusiasm than was necessary. I didn't even realize I was nearly shouting in his face until Patty Sue warned me by stepping on my foot. Whoops. Calm down, Rosemary. "But he... umm... he actually told us he was feeling very...."

"Under the weather! He was feeling under the weather!" Margie supplied like we were playing a game of fill-in-the-blanks.

"The poor thing caught a bad case of the flu," Doris said smoothly. She was fixing her makeup in front of the mirror, looking cool as a cucumber. But I could see her hands were trembling as she tried to layer on her mascara.

"You know, all these people around. Coughing all over the place and whatnot," Patty Sue said, twirling her hands around in the air. "He wasn't looking very good last night. So maybe he'll be skipping this one."

"Spewing out on both ends too. It was quite a sight to behold," Margie very helpfully added. Doris and Patty Sue gave her the side eye while I tried not to laugh.

We may have oversold it a little since his face twisted into a grimace. "Alright, alright. I get it already. No need for all the gross details. Geez." He marched right back out of the room and started hollering for the assistant director, Jeffrey.

"Whew. That was close," Doris breathed a sigh of relief as soon as the door closed.

"We really have to work on our storytelling skills," Patty Sue said, giving Margie another side eye.

"What? We had to make it believable, didn't we?"

The door to the dressing room opened again, and Rick popped his head inside. He stared at us for a few beats, looking unsure of himself. I could tell we were all thinking of the big, ugly elephant in the room.

"Um... hey. You guys will be on in a bit. So maybe you could head over backstage, so we can put in your earpieces?"

"Of course! We'll be there in a bit!" I answered in a voice that was way too cheery. I really had to get a grip on myself.

Behind the thick velvet curtain, Rick started connecting my in-ear monitors. As he untangled the thin cables, he started with some small talk, which wasn't really small talk. "Yesterday was crazy, huh?"

That was the understatement of the century. "I still can't believe that it actually happened. When I woke up this morning, I thought it was just a nasty dream."

"I just... I can't believe it myself, Rosemary. He's gone just like that."

The events from yesterday started playing in my mind again. It had been on an endless loop since last night. This was *not* good for my stomach at all. "You went outside to call for help, right?"

He plugged in a couple of cables and checked the settings on his consoles. "Yeah. I called for emergency services."

"In the staff quarters? Ian went there to make a call too."

"Oh no. I ran all the way to my own cabin to make the call. I would have used the phone backstage, but it wasn't working."

That was interesting. The crew cabins were a long way off from the music hall. "Did you see anyone else walking around on your way? Maybe you caught someone coming in or out of the hall."

He fiddled at the endless rows of knobs and buttons on the mixing console. "No. The halls and boardwalk were empty. Even the staff weren't around anymore. It was pretty late, after all."

"But no one from the emergency services came, right? That's kind of strange, don't you think?"

"They must have called Captain Doherty directly. I don't really know."

Great. Another dead end. I watched Rick work, his practiced hands flying over the console. Maybe he knew more about the captain than we did. "What do you make of her? The captain?"

"I've worked with her before. Once or twice. She has always kept a tight ship."

I waited for him to say something more, but he was too busy setting up the monitor systems.

"Don't you think this is a teeny tiny bit ridiculous?" I pushed on, dropping my voice to a whisper. "I don't understand the point she's trying to make."

"Neither do I. But I'm just a tech guy, the lowest rung on the totem pole," he said with a little chuckle. "I know better than to make waves, you know what I mean?"

"I... uh... guess so." I nodded even though I wasn't really sure if I agreed with him at all.

He tapped at the microphone, and it gave a little screech. He picked up my electric guitar and started plugging cables to that too.

"Okay, you're good to go, Rosemary," he said with a cute,

dimpled smile. He was such a sweetheart. I felt bad for how the captain spoke to him yesterday.

He was about to turn and leave when I called him back. "Oh, and Rick?"

"Yeah?"

"For the record, you're not just a tech guy. This whole thing wouldn't work without you."

When he smiled again, his dimples looked even deeper. "You're too kind. Have a great show out there!"

Rick disappeared, and I made my way to the microphone standing in front of the stage just as we were announced. Still hidden from view by the massive velvet curtains, my electric guitar dangled from my neck, suddenly feeling very heavy.

I snuck a final look at the girls positioned behind me. Patty Sue was fiddling with the guitar strap on her neck. Margie was biting the nail on her thumb again. Doris was staring straight ahead with a blank look on her face and her drumsticks poised in mid-air.

"Hey!" I hissed at them, and they all snapped to attention. "Focus! We got this, alright?"

On the other side of the curtain, the crowd gave a deafening roar. In an instant, the girls straightened up like zombies come back to life.

Doris shook her shoulders, squaring off like she was about to step into a boxing cage and fight. "We can do this. We can do this."

"Right. We've played big crowds before. This is gonna be a piece of cake," said Patty Sue, as if trying to convince herself. As the crowd chanted louder, her fingers fiddled with the guitar strap even more.

"Four best-selling albums!" the announcer's voice boomed.

"Three months on top of the Billboard Hot 100! One of the bestselling acts of the last decade!"

I gave my hair a final flip, brushing all thoughts of Carl and the captain out of my mind. Adrenaline rushed through my veins, hot and slick like fuel. I was going to set this whole stage on fire.

The curtain started to rise as the announcer's voice boomed again. "Ladies and gentlemen!"

Here we go.

"For the first time aboard The Ovation!"

Here.

"The one..."

We.

"The only..."

Go.

"The Delta Queens!"

The curtain disappeared into the ceiling, and there was nothing but a bright spotlight above me. In the crowd, there was just blackness, save for a few silhouettes in the front row. Even though I couldn't see anything, I felt the crowd's energy thrumming through me like a live wire.

I gripped the microphone with both hands. Doris picked up the beat, slowly at first, the kick drum thumping like a heartbeat. And then I opened my mouth. For a split second, I thought no words would come out.

But when Margie's keyboard started its bright, metallic sound, the lyrics started to spill out of me like lava. Doris blasted through the opening notes with her drums. Four notes on the snare. Four notes on the tom. Right, left, right, left. Patty Sue's bass rumbled and crooned.

On cue, my fingers started to pull at the guitar's strings.

Without thinking, I just let it rip, my voice and my guitar falling perfectly in sync. The first song on our setlist was "Crazy of Us," a rock-heavy banger guaranteed to make the crowd come alive.

I looked across the stage. This time I was able to make out a sea of faces in the throng. Everyone was dancing and jumping to the beat as if the floor was just one massive trampoline.

I threw my head back. Shimmied my shoulders and flipped my hair around. The crowd grew even wilder. I was on fire now, singing with every fiber of my being.

I didn't need to look at the ladies to know that they were right there in the zone with me. We were lost and found in the music. We melded into the song and brought it alive together. The telepathy between us was a secret language only we knew.

The weave of music was hypnotic. And it was all ours. I soaked it in, the screams of the crowd piercing through my earpiece, the rasp in my throat as I belted out the lyrics. The white-hot spotlight felt more like the sun now, and I was a plant bowing in its direction.

This was euphoria. This was the reason why we were here. I struck one last note, belting it out as the crowd chanted for more, more, more. Doris finished it up with a final clash of her cymbals. I struck a pose, arms out and head back in self-offering. Nothing could ever ruin this moment.

I swept my gaze across the crowd and leaned forward to clasp their outstretched hands. My cheeks hurt from smiling so much. Yet something from the corner of my eye caught my attention. A crisp white uniform with golden epaulets.

I turned to look and saw Captain Doherty's scowling face, watching us like a hawk.

Fan News

PATTY SUE

"Wow! You guys were incredible! That was such a great show." Rick came up to us and took out our earpieces. One encore turned into another as the crowd kept chanting for more. The velvet curtains were back down now, but I was still buzzing and jittery from a post-performance high.

"That felt incredible! I wouldn't mind doing that every night!" My guitar strap was soaked with sweat, but it was all worth it. The ladies looked like they were on cloud nine too. There was nothing but happy chatter backstage. Maybe Margie and Doris were right. We should just put this whole Carl debacle thing aside and focus on our cruise ship tour.

"Ladies," came a voice from behind us. It was a distinct New Yorker accent, with a sharp, nasally twang that I would now recognize anywhere.

"Captain Doherty," Doris said amicably. So much for putting it aside. I might have spoken too soon.

"Congratulations. Your show was wonderful," she said. She smiled a little, if you could count lifting one corner of her mouth a millimeter high a smile. Stage crew members were still running around and gathering up equipment. I supposed that was why she was trying to look cordial.

"Thank you for the... kind words. We had a great time performing," Margie answered, her voice just as stilted.

"I'm looking forward to your next shows. I'll be sure I'm present for all of them." This time when she smiled, a few teeth showed. I was reminded of Margie's cat back home, playing around with the rats she caught before devouring them.

"After all," she continued, her eyes laughing. "We have you by the neck now, don't we?"

Her little joke wasn't lost on me. From the corner of my eye, I could see Rosemary gritting her teeth together.

"That's great. We'll be sure to give you a special shoutout when we're on stage," I hit back with just enough sarcasm to hopefully annoy her. I smiled at her, too, for good measure.

"Please do," she challenged. "See you around, ladies. And Rick." She gave us a little nod before disappearing into the crowd. Rick looked like he was sweating through his t-shirt again.

"What a two-faced little...." Rosemary seethed. "Let me at her! No one messes with The Delta Queens! No one!"

We pulled her back before she could race after the captain and give her a good wallop.

"Alright, alright. Let's go outside and get some air," Doris said, nearly dragging Rosemary by the elbow toward the staff exit door and the outer deck of the ship.

It was dark now, with just the moon twinkling in the sky. After the performance, I was pretty sure the sun would still be up. But life on a cruise ship could be disorienting.

"Can you believe that? She's acting like she owns us!" Rosemary gripped the steel railing so hard that her knuckles turned white.

"She kind of does," I said.

"Oh, great. Not you too, Patty Sue."

"Don't you see? She's on a power trip. She's watching us like crazy. I wouldn't be surprised if she's having us followed too. The question is why."

"Do you think she suspects us?" Margie said. She leaned over the railing and watched the churning dark water below.

"That wouldn't seem too far-fetched, given how crazy she's acting. Why would we even murder someone? It doesn't make sense," Rosemary said.

From here, I could hear the loud chatter of the crowd on the other side of the upper deck and the slapping of the waves from down below. Why was Captain Doherty going to such great lengths to keep this a secret?

"She's hiding something," I said. "I'm not sure what, but she's definitely hiding something."

"Hey there!" came a man's voice heading in our direction. Under the small deck lights, I could barely make out his shadow.

Oh, great. What is it now?

He sprinted toward us, and a heavily tattooed young man came into view. He was tall and lanky, with long hair fit for a rockstar.

"Sorry to just intrude like this," he said, bouncing on the balls of his feet like an excited kid. "I'm Ace. You guys were amazing on stage! I'm such a huge fan of yours!"

He had a piercing in his nose and another on his lip. When he talked, I caught a glimpse of silver jewelry. Was his tongue pierced too? I could tell that got Rosemary's attention.

"Oh, thank you. That's too kind," Rosemary said. Her anger from a few minutes ago just dissipated into thin air.

I was just about to tell him that we were about to leave when he said something that sent a shiver down my spine.

"Your technical director is Carl, right?"

Doris did a double take, her green eyes growing wide as dinner plates. "What? How did you know that?"

"A buddy of mine in the lighting department told me he'd be here."

"And you're part of the stage crew as well? Here?" I don't even know why I asked. I'd never seen this man before in my life, and I never forgot a face.

"Heck no." His face morphed into something akin to horror and disgust. "I worked with Carl a few years back. Never again."

Well, this mysterious young man just became a thousand times more interesting. "Why'd you say that?" I prompted.

"Oh, you know. He's a brilliant tech director but a terrible person in general," he said with a lazy shrug of his shoulders. "He pretty much ruined my career." He chuckled after saying this, and I wasn't sure if he was making a joke or not.

"What? What happened?"

He stuffed his hands into his pockets and looked away. "He made life miserable for all of us working for him. Then he badmouthed me to everyone he knew until I couldn't get hired on any other cruise ship."

The girls and I all looked at each other. Nobody was blinking. "I'm so sorry. That's terrible," soothed Rosemary.

"It's not so bad. After I got fired, I moved to Tennessee and started my own band. You guys inspired me so much!"

That was quite a turn of events.

"Aww, shucks. That's so great to hear," Rosemary cooed. If it wasn't dark out, I would have sworn she was blushing.

"I'm here on the cruise with my girlfriend, and lo and behold, I find out my favorite band is playing! I'm telling you, I was first in line for the show. I just really wanted to meet you guys," he gushed. He looked adorable, if not a little paradoxical. This man was all tatted up and pierced all over, but he was looking at us like we were Santa Claus incarnate.

Then Ace looked around and whispered to us. "And just... you know, to tell you to watch out for Carl. Always keep one eye open and all that."

"We'll... we will keep that in mind," Doris said to him. I could tell she was ready to end the conversation right away before it steered into something else.

"Is he here right now?" he asked innocently.

Too late.

"No! No, he's not here!" Margie said quickly. She stepped in front of the exit doors like Carl would come busting out at any moment. "He's... um... he has a cold! No, wait, the flu! He has the flu."

"Ah well. That's probably for the best. He wasn't a fan of me either." His attention snapped back toward us like a rubber band. "I don't suppose I could get your autographs?"

"Of course," I answered immediately. The less he kept talking about Carl, the better it would be. He pulled out a well-worn magazine, a *Vanity Fair* edition from ten years ago, featuring our faces. He took out a Sharpie, and we quickly scribbled our signatures on the lacquered paper.

Were we supposed to tell him that the guy he was warning us about was already dead?

Lurking Around

DORIS

"We should go back," Patty Sue said. This time, she was the one pacing back and forth in our living room.

"Back where?" Margie asked before yawning. She was slouched on the sofa, still in her performance outfit—leopard print pants and a ripped-up black t-shirt. It was a few minutes after midnight, and the post-performance high was starting to disappear.

Patty Sue clenched and unclenched her fists. "To the music hall. We might find some clues we missed before."

"Uh, let's not do that," I shook my head with my eyebrow cocked. "The captain told us to leave it. We're probably on her radar already. And the last thing we need right now is trouble from the authorities."

"She doesn't have to know. We'll be careful," said Rosemary as she smacked a piece of gum. The glitter from her purple jumpsuit was shedding all over the sofa.

"Is this really a good idea?" I wasn't sure if I was saying that because I was being careful or just so exhausted.

"We won't do anything. We'll just look around," Rosemary said with another pop of her gum.

"Besides," Patty Sue added. "It's really late. Bet you ten bucks there won't be anyone around the music hall at this late hour."

Before I could open my mouth to reply, we heard the faint slam of a door in the hallway. It sounded close, like it came from the room beside us. And then there were footsteps. Patty Sue raced to our door to see who it was.

"Ian?" she called after the retreating figure into the hallway. Ian froze in place and then gingerly turned around.

"Ladies? Why are you still up?" Ian looked even worse for wear with dark bags under his eyes and rough scraggly stubble on his face.

"Because we just finished performing. You just disappeared on us back there, by the way," Rosemary said.

"Yeah. What's up with that?" I remembered looking for Ian after our show, but he wasn't backstage like usual. "And where are you headed this late?"

"Me? Oh! I'm... uh... just gonna go get myself a snack. Over at the 24-hour dining hall. I suddenly got a bad case of the midnight munchies, you know?"

There he was, acting so weird again, his face as red as a cherry tomato.

"Where are you guys off to?" he asked, clearly changing the subject.

"Back to the music hall. I forgot my jacket," I said smoothly before it dawned on me that people don't really bring jackets on Caribbean cruises. Lucky me, Ian didn't seem to be paying attention anyway.

"Ah." He started tapping his foot and looking toward the

exit. "Well, don't forget to get out of those costumes. You wouldn't want to get mobbed or anything."

What was up with him? "Yeah... sure thing."

"Well, I really have to go now." He turned around and nearly sprinted out of the corridor. "I'll see you tomorrow, yeah? And great job tonight!" And just like that, Ian was gone.

We stood there staring at one another in confusion before I looked at our clothes, all shiny with glitter and rhinestones. This wasn't really the kind of outfit you wore for sneaking around.

"He's right. We do have to get out of these costumes."

"Look at those metal beams up there," I heard Patty Sue say. Her voice echoed across the vast, empty space of the music hall.

It was bleak and eerie. The cold blast of air from the air conditioning drove shivers down my back. Thank goodness a couple of lights were left turned on backstage.

I looked up where Patty Sue was pointing, and sure enough, there was a catwalk that looked wide enough for a single person to walk on above a grid of thick steel beams suspended over the backstage area.

"Right there. Someone could have climbed up, walked across the catwalk, cut the cables on one of the beams, and caused the lights to fall," Patty Sue deduced. I had to agree that she might not be too far off from the truth. I could have climbed up there easily. Maybe there was a ladder stowed away somewhere.

"Then that means there was someone in the music hall with us while we were practicing, right?" I said.

"I think so. Maybe someone came in through the back door?"

"Then that would mean everyone on the cruise ship is a suspect! Anyone could have come in through that door anytime they wanted," Margie surmised, her face twisted in a look of shock.

"That's true. We can't just go around with a picture of Carl and ask the guests, 'Hey, did you maybe murder this guy?'" I shot back.

"Wait, wasn't Carl yelling at Rick to lock the door backstage before we started?" asked Rosemary. She walked over to a battered wooden door beside the controls and opened it to check. The breeze of the cold night air whooshed in. "This door right here."

"Yes, I remember that too. Rick did lock that door. I heard him do it right before we started the last rehearsal," Patty Sue answered. "Carl was needlessly yelling at the poor guy, as I recall."

"Great. So unless someone came through that door before he locked it, then that brings us down to us four, Monica, and Rick," Margie counted on her fingers. "Ian had left the hall, and if he did come back in, he would have used the main entrance since the back door was closed."

"Monica was close to backstage when we were rehearsing!" Rosemary said suddenly, hitting my arm like she just figured the whole thing out. "I remember she was standing right there toward the side!"

"Do you think she snuck around and climbed up there?" Margie asked as she stared up at the ceiling and toward the rafters. Could Monica have done it? She was a petite thing, after all. I envisioned her walking across the catwalk with the stealth of a gymnast. But why would she even do that?

"Do you remember what she said to us when we first met her? Her real passion is true crime mysteries and thrillers!" hissed Rosemary, her eyes wide and unblinking.

"Well, okay. What does that have to do with anything?" Margie said, still staring up.

"What if... she wanted this to happen? She wanted to be part of a true crime mystery so much that she caused this whole mess in the first place?" Rosemary said.

"That's a bit of a stretch, isn't it? She wouldn't kill a man just so she'd have something new to write," Patty Sue said with an incredulous look on her face.

"I agree with Patty. You're starting to sound a bit like a crazed conspiracy theorist, Rose," I added.

"What then, Doris? It couldn't have been us. We were busy performing."

"That leaves us with Rick. Since Ian had already left," I said.

Rosemary waved me off and shook her head. "That boy wouldn't hurt a fly."

The four of us fell silent as we tried to think. The exhaustion of the day was starting to settle in my bones, and I thought I might fall asleep right there, huddled in a little circle backstage. The faint sound of footsteps from outside pricked at my ears and jolted me awake.

"What was that?" Patty Sue whispered. We all looked at each other for a split second before bolting for the open door.

"Someone's outside," I hissed at Patty Sue. "And you owe me ten bucks."

Rosemary charged outside first. When I stepped out, I caught a petite shadowy figure running away.

"Monica? Monica! Hey!" Rosemary called out at the retreating figure. "I think that was Monica!"

"The journalist Monica?" Margie said. She was squinting in the dark, trying to catch a glimpse, but whoever it was had disappeared around the corner.

"Do you know a hundred other Monicas on this cruise ship?" Rosemary barked. "What are we waiting for? Let's go!"

Thank goodness we had replaced our sky-high heels with comfy Adidas sneakers. I planted my feet on the ground, ready to bolt. It didn't matter that I had just turned thirty-nine recently... I wasn't a high school track star for nothing.

Walk the Plank

MARGIE

"Over there! That-a-way!" Doris was flying down the deck and speeding around corners. My shoes were clomping down on the wood deck, trying to keep up with her. The girl was fast.

But maybe not fast enough for Monica or whoever it was. The mysterious figure was nowhere to be seen. Had they even really seen anyone, or was it just a figment of their imaginations? I wouldn't hold it against them, honestly. We were all exhausted.

"Whoa, I'm getting way too old for this," I panted. The cooler night air was biting into my lungs as I willed my legs to keep going. Thankfully, after what felt like hours of running, Doris started to slow down.

"Dang it! We lost her," she huffed.

"Well, she is a spritely little thing," said Patty Sue, bending over to catch her breath. "Where could she have disappeared to?"

I realized we were in the middle of the promenade deck, near the bow of the ship. It was empty, but a row of deck lights illuminated the walkway, so it wasn't as creepy as the music hall.

Gift shops and restaurants flanked us on both sides, with wooden dining sets and lounge chairs scattered around. If it wasn't for the salty ocean breeze, I would have thought we were right back home in Alabama, wandering around town.

"What in the world was Monica doing back there so late?" Doris said, still panting. "She wasn't supposed to be there, was she?"

"I don't know about you girls, but it's pretty obvious she was sneaking around," said Rosemary with a smug look. "I'm not going to say I told you so, but... I told you so. There's something strange about that girl."

"What is she up to?" Patty Sue said, her shoulders sagging as we walked.

Rosemary couldn't keep still. "What if Captain Doherty hired her to spy on us? What if... what if she was there to eliminate us?"

"What are you even talking about?" I said with a tired groan.

"Think about it, Margie. We were witnesses to Carl's murder. She knows that we know that she was there."

"Now I'm just straight up confused," Doris muttered.

"What if, knock on wood, Monica and Captain Doherty want us to be... permanently quiet?" Rosemary whispered, making a cutthroat gesture with her hand.

"Now that's just crazy talk," I said. "Sure, Monica's a bit quirky, and she talks a mile a minute, but I don't think she's a red-blooded murderer."

"Besides," Doris added, "Not to brag or anything, but if we all disappeared tomorrow, it would be a pretty damn big deal. And she's a journalist. She knows that."

She was right, we weren't the hotshots we used to be, but

The Delta Queens were still well known in the south. If we were all "eliminated" all of a sudden, that would cause some big waves in the news.

"Wait a second," said Doris. "Do you think she heard us back there? When we were speculating and talking about how she might have caused this whole thing in the first place. What if she just ran away because we hurt the poor girl's feelings?"

"Alright, alright," Rosemary surrendered. "Say, it ain't Monica. Then who did it?"

"Let's not discount that handsome Ace guy we just talked to. He had a bone to pick with Carl," Patty Sue interjected. "What if he snuck in through the backstage door before Rick had a chance to lock it?"

"Then why did he tell us about his past with Carl if he killed him? That would have been an incredibly idiotic move on his part," Doris said, shaking her open palms in the air.

I looked around and realized we were walking down an unfamiliar carpeted corridor. The rooms in this area were rather large, with shiny gold name tags on the door. "Hey, where are we? Is this the staff quarters?" We had obviously wandered into the area of the ship designated for the most senior and important staff.

"Wait a star-spangled minute," whispered Patty Sue. "This is Carl's room."

She pointed to a wooden door with a golden plaque hanging on it. *Carl Tanner, Entertainment Technical Director*, it said.

"I wonder if anyone has been inside since he..." I said, trailing off. Saying the word 'died' out loud felt like chalk in my mouth.

"Probably not," Rosemary said. "We're the only ones who know he's... you know. Us, Rick, Ian, Monica, and the captain."

Patty Sue turned to Doris, a slow smirk forming on her face. "Are you thinking what I'm thinking?"

Doris looked at her blankly before realization set in, and she started shaking her head. "Oh no. No, no, no. Don't even dare."

"What? What are you talking about?" I asked. Rosemary looked just as confused as I was.

"Think about it," said Patty Sue, jabbing her finger toward the door. "If he has enemies on this cruise ship, we'll surely find clues in there."

Doris sighed. "If we get caught, we'll get cooked and deep fried."

"There's no one around."

"Like no one was around back at the music hall, Patty Sue? Yet surprise, surprise, Monica was there sneaking around," Doris quipped.

Patty Sue took a deep breath. I still didn't know what they were talking about. "Listen, Doris. The faster we get to the bottom of this, the faster we can put this behind us. Aren't you just a teeny tiny bit curious?"

Doris's mouth lifted at the corners. "You're only saying that because you know I'm the only one who can break into locked places."

Only then did it click for me. Doris taught herself how to pick locks in high school so she could sneak into the music room after hours to practice on the school's one and only drum kit. And she never got caught.

"Guilty as charged," Patty Sue answered with a smirk like she knew she had already won. "You are curious, though. I can see it in your eyes. You want to figure this out just as much as we do."

Doris rolled her eyes, but she was still smiling. She crouched down and eyeballed the lock like she was sizing it up. "Maybe I do. But that doesn't change the fact that Captain Doherty could make us walk the plank if she finds out what we're up to."

"Well, we didn't do anything wrong," said Rosemary. "Why should we be scared? They're the ones with all the weird, mysterious secrets. We just want to figure out what's really going on."

Doris sighed again.

"Now go on ahead and work your magic," Rosemary chided her.

"Yeah. C'mon, Doris. You got this," I added.

"Fine, fine. But I'm gonna need this," Doris said before plucking a hairpin right out of Patty Sue's long dark locks.

She pulled apart the bobby pin so that it turned into a long, flat metal piece. Then she stuck the flat end inside the keyhole, carefully pushing left and right and slightly bending the end of the pin. It wasn't long before we heard a loud click. Doris turned to us with a Cheshire cat grin, eyes gleaming.

"Alright, girls. We're in."

Dangerous Act

ROSEMARY

"Whoa. Look at this place!" The room wasn't a luxury deluxe stateroom by any means—it was still a crew cabin after all—but it was still a really nice room. There were two small porthole windows and a full-sized bed. A small sitting area was situated by a kitchen-like space with a microwave and mini-fridge.

"Can you believe this? He's got this huge bed all to himself while we're slumming it in tiny twin beds! I wouldn't mind living here, that's for darn sure."

Margie opened the door to his bathroom and let out an appreciative whistle. "And look at the size of this shower! You can bathe an elephant in here!"

Doris pinched the bridge of her nose. "Can we just focus on clues, please? And no one touch anything! We don't want our fingerprints all over this place."

"Alright, alright. Don't get your panties in a bunch," I said, even though I really wanted to flop down on that huge soft bed and take a little nap.

"We're in and out in five minutes, okay?" Doris said. "Five

minutes! The last thing we need is someone walking in here and catching us."

"Relax. Who's gonna come in here? Carl's ghost?"

"Rosie!" Margie yelped. "Don't make jokes like that!"

"Focus, everyone!" Doris growled at us before turning to Patty Sue. "What are we looking for exactly?"

Patty Sue scratched her head and looked around. "Notes? Letters? Maybe someone already threatened him."

"Alright, that shouldn't be hard. At least he's neat."

I pulled down the sleeves of my sweater to cover up my hands, then pulled open the cabinets and rifled through the shelves. There was nothing but cereal boxes and bags of trail mix. He had a single bowl, a single plate, and a slew of plastic silverware in there. I reckoned he wasn't one for hosting guests.

I moved to the closet, which was also significantly bigger than ours. When I turned the knob, the last thing I expected was a waterfall of leather bags bursting through the door. I gave out a loud shriek before Doris ran over and clamped her hand over my mouth.

"Shhhh, Rosie! Are you trying to get us in trouble?"

"Swa-ree," I said, my words muffled from behind her hand. "I was surprised."

A dozen or more bags had fallen on the floor. It looked like I was standing in a sea of slick, shiny leather. There were designer handbags in different shapes and sizes and colors.

"What in the name of..." Patty Sue mumbled. She plucked one up with a covered hand and squinted at it like she was studying an alien life form.

What in the world is going on? Prada. Chanel. Louis Vuitton. Why does Carl have all these women's handbags stuffed in his closet?

"This is so bizarre," Doris said. "I have never even seen Carl walk around with a backpack. He looked more like a stuff-everything-in-your-pockets kind of guy."

"Maybe he's a collector? And these bags are vintage?" said Margie. She picked up a black Prada bag. It was nylon with a fancy gold chain. "Oooh, this one is nice. I bet it costs an arm and a—"

"Hold on a flippin' second," interrupted Patty Sue, her face contorting with slight disgust. "These aren't real designer bags!"

"What? How would you even know?"

"My mom loved collecting designer bags. She taught me a thing or two. These are very good imitations, but they're not the real thing. Not by a long shot." Patty Sue carefully opened the Yves Saint Laurent bag in her hand and showed us the inside.

"Most designer bags will have an inside tag with the brand name and a serial number on it. The inside tags are either hand-stitched or stamped into the leather. Look at the stitching on this one. It's wonky and uneven."

I studied the tag. She was right; the stitching was slanted and hurried. And the logo wasn't even placed in the center.

"Also, real designer bags have sturdy metal hardware, and fake designer bags will use plastic or cheap metal." She picked up a gorgeous, quilted Chanel bag and pointed to the inter-locked CC logo dangling from the zipper. I reached out and touched it. Even with my hands covered, I could tell it wasn't solid but hollow. It was even beginning to chip.

"Even the lining inside is all wrong." Patty Sue sniffed the leather fabric of the Yves Saint Laurent bag she was holding and made a face. "And that is definitely not what real leather smells like."

"Incredible. So, these are all counterfeits?" I looked at the handbags around my feet. The fine Italian leather I was admiring just minutes ago now looked cheap and dirty.

"Why in the world would Carl have all these counterfeit handbags? Does he sell these to the guests? It doesn't make sense!" Doris huffed in frustration.

"Maybe something else around here can answer that for us," I said. With a new surge of adrenaline, I whipped open the drawers under his desk one by one. A few pencils. Some rolled-up socks. Aviator sunglasses. It wasn't until I reached the bottom drawer that I found something interesting. Envelopes and letters. Lots and lots of letters.

"Ah-ha! I found something! Take a look at this."

The letters were handwritten in swirly cursive. They all started the same way, *My dearest Carl* and ended with *Yours always, Natty.* "Awww. Love letters. That's so cute," Margie cooed.

"Rick said Carl didn't have a girlfriend," Doris recalled. "What do the letters say?"

I stared at the loopy writing. The letters started out the same way, with something about how she missed him and thought about him all the time. A little cheesy if you asked me.

"Maybe he kept the whole thing private," Patty Sue said as she rifled through another drawer. "Oh, look. This must be her." She held up a picture of a pretty woman posing at the beach. The words "Wish you were here" were written on the back.

"What a sweet-looking thing," said Margie. "She's pretty as a peach." The woman had gorgeous shiny long black hair and a radiant smile.

"I bet she and Carl made a nice-looking couple," I said. "Is she wondering where Carl is right now? Is she waiting for a letter that will never arrive? It's just... so sad."

The faint sound of footsteps from outside broke our reverie. After a second or two, the sound disappeared. But that was enough to make Doris nearly pull her hair out.

"Okay, okay. We've stayed here long enough. I'm as nervous as a long-tailed cat in a room full of rockin' chairs. Let's get out of here. Now!"

As we scooped up the fake designer bags and stuffed them back in the closet, it dawned on me that we weren't any closer to an answer now than when we had started.

Making Waves

PATTY SUE

"Everyone clear on the plan?" Doris asked as she slathered sunscreen on her face, putting on so much that she ended up looking like a ghost.

"Yes," Rosemary drawled. "You've repeated it six times. Go to the art auction at the onboard gallery, look for Monica, and then follow her around like she followed us around."

"Then what do we do?" Margie asked innocently.

"We corner her. Find out what she knows. She's hiding something, I can tell."

I had to admit, what Doris recommended didn't leave us much to go on, but it wasn't like we had a laundry list of suspects. Even if Monica wasn't guilty, I still wanted to know why she was following us the other night.

"How do you even know she's going to be there?" Margie said.

"I don't," Doris answered. "It's a calculated guess. She's a journalist, remember? She'd want to know about all the main events happening on the cruise ship. Where's my hat? I need my hat."

"We'll just be walking around outside. We're not taking a trip to the sun," Rosemary said with a snort. Doris ignored her while she rooted around her bag. She found her massive floppy sunhat and plopped it on her head.

"Remember, we don't want to draw any attention to ourselves." Doris gave Rosemary the once-over, pointedly looking at her mini skirt and tight leopard print blouse.

"What? I'm not going to do anything." Rosemary's eyes twinkled with innocence, but her mouth curved into a mischievous smile.

"Don't go chasing after the first hunk you see, okay? The last thing we need is people recognizing us."

"I make no such promises, darlin'."

"Oh, for Pete's sake, Rosemary. Can't you keep it in your pants for one day?"

They could keep yapping at each other all day. I opened the door and ushered them out before they really went at each other's throats. "Okay! Let's just... get a move on, shall we?"

Rosemary put on her oversized shades and strutted down the hallway, her strapless heels clicking on the bottoms of her feet. In my Bermuda shorts with a matching crop top, I would fit in with the crowd just fine, just like Doris wanted us to do. Rosemary, however, would probably be mistaken for a runway model of some sort. So much for being incognito.

The boardwalk thrummed with activity. There was a crowd playing shuffleboard and a gaggle of children running around and screaming. A few feet away was the pool deck, where sunbathers on lounge chairs were packed in like sardines. A group of young men was playing pool volleyball, their skin gleaming under the bright sun. I hurried everyone along before

Rosemary could get distracted by the muscles and six-pack abs on display.

"There it is! The art gallery!" I said with a little too much enthusiasm. We walked inside an exhibition hall where dozens of paintings were up on display. There were a lot of people milling around, although the crowd wasn't as big as the one over at the pool deck.

"I think it's best if we stick together," Doris whispered. We moved through the crowd in a huddle, like a pack of baby gazelles in the wild looking out for predators.

The auction had already started. A man was up on stage, eagerly presenting a framed painting of wild horses running across a field. I craned my neck as inconspicuously as possible, looking for a young woman with thick-rimmed eyeglasses.

"Dang it, I don't see her anywhere."

"Maybe she's not here after all," said Rosemary. "Maybe she's over at the pool watching the volleyball game."

"Can it, Rosie," hissed Doris.

"Hey, you never know."

"Over there! I see her!" came Margie's voice. People started placing bids on the horse painting, lifting their paddles up in the air as the auctioneer shouted out the ever-increasing highest bid. But I couldn't see Monica anywhere.

"Where? Where?"

Margie started walking quickly, and we followed suit. "Over there by the painting of the droopy tulips." We barged through a group of ladies sipping champagne, and one of them gave us the stink eye. I still couldn't see Monica, though.

"Oh no. She's leaving!" said Margie. Only then did I catch a glimpse of Monica's head as she walked toward the exit.

"Shoot. Okay, let's go, let's go, girls. Let's pick up the pace!"

Before I knew it, we were out of the exhibition hall and speed walking across the boardwalk. Monica headed toward the pool deck, stopped abruptly, and then looked around.

"Ha! I told you she wanted to watch the volleyball game," Rosemary said with a smug look on her face. Her face brightened as soon as she saw a nicely built man come flying out of the pool to hit the ball back over the net. Doris was about to fire back a retort when Monica started to move again.

"Guess not," Doris smirked. Monica kept walking, and we trailed along behind her, weaving through the bikini-clad crowd until we reached the promenade deck.

I couldn't help but notice Monica kept looking around, a concerned expression on her face. I didn't think she was on to us, but it looked like she was constantly looking for someone. "Why is she acting so weird?"

"I think she's following someone," Margie said. The crowd was so thick that it was hard to tell for sure. Among the throng, I spotted a familiar-looking face a few feet away from us, with jet black hair and oversized aviators perched on the nose. And that bomber jacket.

"Is that... Ian?"

"Crap on a cracker. That is Ian," Doris mumbled. She adjusted her floppy hat so that it covered most of her face. It didn't seem to matter, though, because Ian hadn't seen us. He looked distracted too. I looked around for our original target, Monica, only to find her staring intently at Ian, the sunlight reflecting off her eyeglasses.

Rosemary seemed to have read my mind because she glared in Monica's direction. "First, she follows us around. Then she follows Ian. Oh, this girl is trouble, I'm telling you."

"Was Ian in the art gallery too? Why in the world would he

be there?" Doris wondered. Apparently, we had been so focused on looking for Monica that we had barely noticed Ian was there.

Only a few seconds went by before Monica's head disappeared among the crowd. "Hey! Where'd she go?"

I stood on my tiptoes to look, but waves and waves of people were walking by. It didn't help that a bunch of kids on a sugar high were running around, virtually trapping us in a circle.

"Where did she go? Dang it, why is that girl so fast?"

"Down there! I see her!" Margie pointed toward the lower deck. "And there's Ian."

Ian strode toward the railing with Monica a good forty feet away. When Ian stopped walking, Monica kept her distance, taking a seat on a nearby lounge chair and hiding herself under the massive umbrella.

We eased ourselves away from the crowd and the screaming kids and positioned ourselves by the railing. From the deck above, we had a pretty good vantage point, although it was still hard to see. "We're so far away. Can't we get any closer?"

"Not unless we want Monica to see us," said Rosemary.

"Hold on, I have something," said Margie. She pulled out a pair of binoculars from her large tote bag. Thank goodness Margie was a girl scout-Mary Poppins hybrid. She positioned herself by the horizontal spindles on the railing and used the binoculars to focus closer on the action.

"What do you see?"

"Nothing. Ian's just standing there." Ian was leaning on the railing and looking out at the ocean. If anything, he looked like a typical tourist admiring the view. Ten minutes later, a bald, heavyset man walked up near him. He also leaned on the railing. Probably another tourist waiting for the sunset views.

"Ian's talking to someone," Margie said. "That bald guy over there. I don't think we've seen him before."

"The one with the chinos and loafers? He looks like my elementary school science teacher," Rosemary commented. "And they're just talking?"

"He's probably a new friend Ian met on the cruise. You know Ian... he could make friends with Ebenezer Scrooge," Doris said.

Even though we were quite a distance away, I could see the vague motions of Ian nodding his head and the bald guy's mouth moving.

"Can you make out what they're saying?" I asked Margie.

"I... I don't think so. They're talking way too fast."

"Ugh. Another dead end," sighed Rosemary. "Monica must be kicking herself too."

Margie's brows furrowed, and she let out a hum.

"What is it?"

"Now Ian looks... upset," said Margie.

If I squinted hard in their direction, I could make out a frown flickering across Ian's face and his right hand pinching his fingers together. "Small? He's saying... something's small. A mouse? Is he talking about a mouse?"

The bald guy's face was sour with annoyance, and he started to make big gestures with his hands, motioning to his head.

"Thinking? The thinker? A skull?" Doris guessed.

"This is the weirdest game of charades I've ever played," Rosemary said with a roll of her eyes.

"Money," Margie said. She was gripping the binoculars so tight that her knuckles were turning white. "Ian's saying something about money. He keeps repeating the word."

Sure enough, their movements became more and more

aggressive. Ian looked like he was shouting now, and a passerby looked at them funny.

"Oh, dear. He's saying, 'where's my money?'"

Even from our position on the next deck, they were beginning to look like quite the spectacle. "What? Why would Ian ask him that?"

"Oh no. Are they going to fight?" Doris mumbled.

Sure enough, the bald guy gave Ian a shove. Ian's nose flared with rage, and his hands were clenched into fists.

"Holy mackerel! This is bad. We have to get down there and stop them." My eyes were still glued on them, and my feet were ready to bolt.

Ian tried to shove the man back in retaliation, but the bald guy didn't budge an inch. Their voices started rising in pitch though we couldn't quite make out the words.

"I'm not a lip reader, but I detect a few choice curse words being thrown around."

"Yep. We best get down there before they draw a crowd. Let's go, girls," Doris said. I could tell she was trying to stay calm, but her voice shook as she started looking for a way down.

Even in our haste, I heard Rosemary mumble, "So much for keeping a low profile."

Woman Overboard

DORIS

"Ian! Ian!" We were supposed to stay quiet, but we managed to start screaming and hollering as soon as we reached the lower deck.

"Get off me, punk!" I heard the bald guy say before shoving Ian back into the railing. His ribs made a loud banging sound against the metal, and his sunglasses fell down his nose.

Ian lunged back toward him, grabbing the collar of his shirt and trying to take him down. The bald guy, however, was built like a sturdy steel safe. Ian looked like a tall twig next to him. "Thief! Give me my money back! You better watch your—"

"Ian!"

Ian turned his head at the sound of my voice, his dark brown eyes still blazing. When he saw us, his face morphed into comical shock, his mouth forming into an "O" shape. "Girls? What are you... what are you doing here?"

"What are we doing here?" I asked in disbelief. "What the heck are you doing wrestling around with this guy?"

Ian suddenly let go of his grip on the other guy's shirt. "Oh!

It was just a... little misunderstanding." Then he smoothed the bald guy's shirt while he just stood frozen in place. "This is Stan. We're... good... good friends."

I squinted at him. "If that's how you treat your friends, I'd hate to see what you do to your enemies."

"We were just..." Ian said, chuckling a little. He placed his arm over the bald guy's wide shoulders. "Just talking. You know, clowning around. Right, Stan?"

"Yeah, we were... just watching this wrestling match on TV," Stan mumbled, rubbing the back of his neck and avoiding any eye contact with us.

"Exactly." Another dry chuckle from Ian. "Got a little... carried away, that's all." He looked around at the small crowd watching us. They were probably waiting for a fight. "Nothing to see here, folks." Ian reached over and patted the other guy's shoulder like he would pat a dog's head.

"You people have *got* to be kidding me," came an exasperated voice from nearby. It was Monica. She was standing nearby, away from her perch on the lounge chair, like she wanted a good view of the ruckus. "What the *heck* are all of you up to?"

Rosemary jutted her chin out in defiance. "Oh, we're not answering a darn thing, missy," she said, stepping forward to get right into Monica's face. "Why don't you mind your own beeswax? You think we don't know what you're up to? Nothing gets past The Delta Queens. We're like Miss Marple, you know. Only younger and hotter."

"If you're not hiding anything, then you mind telling me what all of you are doing here?"

"What *we're* doing? Well, what are *you* up to, young lady? Sneaking around all hours of the night. You think you're the only one here with investigative skills?" Rosemary fired back.

Monica's mouth jutted open like she couldn't believe Rosemary just said that. Then she scoffed and crossed her arms. She was trying to look like she had the upper hand, but I could tell she was somewhat terrified of Rosemary. "Well, from where I'm standing, you're just sounding more and more suspicious. I have half a mind to—"

From the corner of my eye, I could see the crowd gathered by the deck parting like the Red Sea. And breezing down the stairs in her immaculate uniform was Captain Doherty, the whiteness of her clothes looking like they could blind somebody. She was smiling and waving at the crowd of onlookers as if she was Miss Alabama 1989.

Oh great... just when I thought things couldn't get any worse.

"Why is it always you and your motley crew?" She showed off her dazzling white teeth as she talked, but the smile didn't reach her eyes. It never did.

"Captain! Um... hi," Ian stammered. "How are ya? Great day we're having, huh?"

Captain Doherty looked around at the crowd slowly dispersing. Once they were out of earshot, she tucked her hands in front of her and smiled again. But her eyes were sharp as flints. "What are you doing exactly?"

"Erm... nothing. Just, you know, hanging out. Enjoying the nice sun and... you know, the views and all that," Ian answered. He dropped his arm off the bald guy's shoulders.

"Are you doing what I think you're doing?"

"What? We're not doing anything!" Rosemary scoffed incredulously. "Can't a bunch of people hang out and watch the sunset?"

Captain Doherty's mouth turned into a small line. "You

think I don't see you running around and creating a ruckus wherever you go? Going back to the music hall after hours?"

She was looking at us one by one. I stifled a gulp. I willed my face not to move or show any emotion, or else she might pounce on me. Did she also know that we broke into Carl's room? I felt my entire body breaking into a sweat.

She glanced at me. "You want to know what happened, don't you?"

"No," I said, forcing a weak chuckle. "We don't... care. We've forgotten all about it, to be honest."

The captain took a deep breath and smiled again, still mindful of the people milling about the deck.

"Do you see me running around like a headless chicken? Trying to get my grubby paws into something that's not my business?" she asked. When no one answered her rhetorical question, she glared at us. I was ready for laser beams to start shooting out of her eyes.

"Erm... no, ma'am. No," I managed to stutter.

"Exactly. And have you forgotten what we talked about?"

We all stayed quiet; everyone pressed together like we were creating a human shield. Stan was still there, looking more and more confused by the second. He didn't dare say a word, though.

"I think you have. I think you've forgotten," she said slowly. She still kept smiling, showing off those perfect teeth.

"No. No, we haven't forgotten," Ian said, some steel coming back to his voice. "I'm sorry. We're all sorry. This won't happen again, I assure you."

The captain sighed deeply. "Too late. You can all say goodbye to your bonus check."

I felt everyone around me stiffen as we held our breath in anticipation of worse things to come.

"It's a shame too. The higher-ups were feeling very generous toward the staff this year," Captain Doherty continued. "And by the way, I'm not signing off on any media coverage for your band."

"What?" Monica exclaimed. "You can't do that! My piece is about The Delta Queens."

"Well, that's too bad." Her voice was like honey, sickeningly sweet. "Maybe you can move to another line of work? Perhaps writing crossword puzzles for gossip rags would best suit you."

Then she turned back to us, laser-focused like she knew she was going to win. "What's that saying? Bad press is better than no press? Well, looks like you won't have to worry about either of those."

"You can't do that! That's preposterous," Rosemary said with a growl.

"Oh, can't I? I wouldn't be so sure of that. Meanwhile, you'll keep performing until I say so. Like my little dancing monkeys."

With how Rosemary was looking around, I could tell she was wondering if she could just deck this woman and get away with it. I gripped her arm tightly, my fingers clawing past her blouse and into her skin.

Captain Doherty turned to leave, but not without flashing us another one of her dazzling, fake smiles. "Your downfall is inevitable, ladies. Why don't you just... prepare for it?" Then she climbed up the stairs and disappeared.

I let go of Rosemary's arm, her fury radiating through her clothes.

"You should've let me go after her, Doris. So she knows who she's messing with."

My knees felt weak, and I found myself leaning on the railing for support. All I could think about were my daughter's big blue eyes staring up at me. I was supposed to be her rock.

"What's the point? We're done."

Jacuzzi Confessions

MARGIE

"Good night, everyone!" Rosemary's voice boomed from the mike, and the crowd answered with a deafening cheer. The vibrations in the air hummed through my seat at the keyboard all the way to the tips of my fingers. "Hope y'all had a great time! We'll see you at our next show!"

We moved to the front of the stage and waved to the crowd. The music hall was filled to the brim, and everyone was jumping. We held hands and took our bows.

"Oh, great," Rosemary muttered from the side of her mouth and right into my ear. "Captain Cruella de Vil is here."

Oh, great indeed. My eyes scanned the area, looking for a woman wearing a white uniform and a scowl. And there she was, sticking out like a sore thumb among the happy crowd. I felt Doris's shoulders sag.

"Just smile and wave, ladies. Just smile and wave," I muttered back. I raised my hand and started waving like an excited little kid. *Captain Doherty and her sour face can go fly a kite.*

When the velvet curtain went down, the atmosphere

changed almost instantly. My smile faded away, and I just wanted to take a nap. "Is it bad that I want this cruise to end already?"

I thought this would be a fun work trip—all sunsets, piña coladas, and sold-out shows. Not murders and crimes and angry ship captains looking over our shoulders.

"Maybe we should just make a swim for it," Rosemary said. This was a year-long gig on the cruise ship, and we had an iron-clad contract, so it didn't look like we would be getting out of this anytime soon. Not legally, at least.

"And go where? I wouldn't be surprised if that woman has spies all over the world," Doris scoffed as she puttered around with the wires of her earpiece.

The guy with the Tom Selleck mustache came up to us again, waving a clipboard at my face. "Hey, you guys ever heard anything from Carl?"

Doris's hand froze near her ear. "What? No. Why would we... why would we hear anything?"

"He's been MIA for several days now. I tried to check up on him in his room, but no one's answering," mustache guy said. His brow was etched with concern. "That's not like him."

Patty Sue gave him a pat on the arm. It was supposed to be a comforting gesture, but I'm pretty sure she just wanted him to leave. "If we hear anything, we'll let you know right away."

I thought he would ask more questions and grill us, but he just gave a brisk nod and walked away.

Behind me, I heard someone let out a loud exhale. It was Rick. I didn't even know he was there.

"Every time someone mentions his name, I go into panic mode." He was starting to break out into a sweat again. I turned around to let him unclip my earpiece.

"You know what? I don't even want to talk about it anymore," I told him. "I wish we could just forget about this whole nightmare."

"You and me both. Every time I come backstage, it's like it's happening all over again," he said, his breath on my back making me shiver.

"Can we just talk about something else? Like your family, maybe? How's your family doing?"

He moved in front of me and untangled some more wires. "My family," he repeated slowly like he was testing the words in his mouth.

"Yeah. Don't you have a wife? Any kids?"

Rick suddenly looked lost in thought, his eyes glazing over. "I have a wife, yeah. She's back home in Florida."

"And how's she handling the distance? It's not easy, I imagine."

It wasn't hard to miss the way his jaw hardened. "It's... a lot of work."

"Don't worry," I said, trying to cheer him up. "You'll see her soon. And it'll be like no time ever passed."

"Yeah, maybe," he said, his face still gloomy. After he finished removing my wires, he turned toward us.

"Say, you ladies want to get a drink after this? The crew bar has some good happy hour specials."

"Oh, I think we'll have to pass, Ricky dear," Rosemary said as she took off her makeup. "I have a better idea, girls. Why don't we hit the pool? Have fun for a change?"

"You're just saying that to ogle at the guys in swimwear," Doris said with a smirk.

Rosemary grinned, her face brightening at the thought. "You know me too well."

* * *

"Ah, this is the life." I was up to my neck in the ship's fancy jacuzzi, jets of water pulsing and whirring around us. The sun was hot, and the strawberry margaritas were nice and cool. I could get used to this.

"You do have some good sound ideas, Rosie," said Doris between sips of her drink. I doubt Rosemary heard a word of what we said since she was so engrossed in watching a group of guys hanging around in the pool.

We were so busy relaxing that we didn't notice a young woman take a seat on the edge of the jacuzzi, dipping her legs in until the water splashed against her knees.

"Monica?"

It was her, with her thick eyeglasses and small, shy smile. She was wearing a bright yellow halter top and blue swim shorts.

Rosemary slid down her sunglasses to get a better look and then groaned. "Oh, great. There goes our relaxing afternoon."

"I... I have to tell you guys something," Monica said, shyer than I'd ever heard her before. She pushed her eyeglasses up the bridge of her nose.

"Come here to gloat?" Rosemary sighed. "We get it, okay? Our investigation went nowhere."

"I did a background check on Stan," she blurted out.

"What? Who?"

"The guy who was with Ian the other day, remember? They were wrestling by the deck?"

Doris put down her drink. "You did a background check? Why would you even do that?"

Patty Sue's eyes brightened with curiosity. She wiggled closer to Monica. "What did you find?"

Monica looked around, checking to see if anybody was within earshot. Then she leaned toward us and whispered, "He is a convicted felon. He has a record of smuggling counterfeit goods. Luxury bags, mostly."

"A record of what?" Rosemary said incredulously.

I felt my jaw fall open. *Did she just say counterfeit goods? Luxury bags? That didn't have anything to do with what we saw in Carl's room, right?*

"That's... oh!" Rosemary exclaimed. With the way her eyes widened, it looked like she had just arrived at the same train of thought as I did.

When Patty Sue and I exchanged furtive glances with Rosemary, Monica was watching us with big curious eyes.

"What? What is it?"

"Nothing," Patty Sue squeaked out. "It's weird, that's all."

Monica narrowed her eyes at us. "You guys know something! I know you do!"

"Look, why did you come to us with this information?" Doris asked her, turning the tables before she could interrogate us. "I thought you were suspicious of us."

"Well, yes, a tiny bit." Her fingers started to pick at her nails. It must be another nervous habit. "It's just... I don't know who else to tell. And I know you ladies are sniffing around too. Maybe we could team up? Five heads are better than one and all that."

She sounded earnest and sincere, but she couldn't even look us in the eye. Was she scared we were going to reject her? Or make fun of her? Suddenly, our theories of her being a suspect didn't make much sense anymore.

"Fine," Rosemary sighed. "But you have to swear that you'll keep this to yourself."

Monica's face lit up. "Who else am I gonna tell? The captain? She's not exactly my biggest fan right now."

"Okay, okay," said Patty Sue. She took a deep breath and then confessed, "A few days ago, we broke into Carl's room."

"What? That's insane! Why did you..." Monica sputtered. Rosemary looked at her with a glare that could wither flowers.

Monica took a deep breath, pinched her nose, and smiled. "It's... fine. I'm not judging. Please continue."

We told her about what we found in Carl's room, especially the closet stuffed with fancy designer bags that were all counterfeits.

"Now that you mentioned Stan, it all makes sense. Maybe Carl was involved in the smuggling racket. And that's what got him killed," Doris said.

My mind flashed back to Ian's face flashing with rage on that deck. "But why would Stan be fighting with Ian? Could he be involved too?"

"I don't know about that," said Patty. "Ian comes from a well-off family. Why would he need to smuggle counterfeit purses?"

"Maybe he bought one of those counterfeit bags and got really angry when he realized it was a fake?" I suggested.

"But fighting in public? That's a bit of an overreaction, don't you think?" Rosemary asked. "And I've never seen Ian that angry before."

There was something we weren't seeing here. Like one piece of the puzzle was missing from the box.

"We know Carl is involved. Stan could be the ringleader or the main smuggler. And it hurts to say this out loud... but Ian might have something to do with it too." Doris listed them out on her fingers. "It definitely makes you wonder, who else?"

Who else? Who else had the most to gain? Most importantly, who would have the most to lose if word of this got out?

I splashed my hand down in the jacuzzi, the spray of water almost getting into our drinks. "I've got it!"

"Hey! Watch the drinks, Margie!" Rosemary exclaimed.

"Captain Doherty! She's in on it too."

"Her?" Monica said. "But she's a Ms. Goody Two-shoes girl scout."

"Think about it. Why doesn't she want us to investigate?" I pressed.

Was this it? Was this the missing puzzle piece we were looking for all this time?

"Maybe there's a whole smuggling operation on board the cruise ship. And she's the kingpin. Or queen pin. Whatever. And she'll do everything in her power to keep things quiet. Heck, maybe it was her who ordered Carl's killing!" Rosemary said, eyes bulging from her head.

"Oh, this is interesting. Very, very interesting." I could see Monica's brain whirring, her journalist's instinct kicking in.

Things were starting to fall in place, and I felt giddy with excitement. Patty's eyes were gleaming. Rosie couldn't sit still. Doris, meanwhile, suddenly looked very queasy.

Monica kicked her feet below the water. She was smiling like she had just won the lottery. Or a Pulitzer Prize. Or both.

"Buckle up, ladies. Looks like we're in for a wild ride."

High Roller

ROSEMARY

"Why are we doing this again?" Margie stood in front of Ian's door, staring intently at the patterns on the wood.

"The only way we can find out what's really going on is by confronting Ian," I told her. Still, I couldn't bring myself to knock on the door myself.

"Ugh. Confronting is such an ugly word."

"We'll just talk to him. It's no big deal." I didn't like confronting him either, but no one was going to do the dirty work for us.

"He might feel like we're ganging up on him. This is Ian we're talking about. He's been with us since we started," Margie said. "Remember how he'd drive us all around Jefferson County in his beat-up old van, trying to get us to our gigs on time?"

Patty Sue piped up. "Look, we're not going to lock him up in a room and interrogate him. We're just here to talk."

"Alright, alright." Margie took a deep breath and started to knock. "Ian? Ian, open up."

There was silence on the other side. No sound of footsteps or furniture creaking.

"Ian? It's us. Open up." Patty Sue pounded on the door, loud enough that the walls shook. Still, nothing.

"Maybe he's asleep? If we knock any louder, the neighbors will throw a fit, though," I said.

Patty Sue turned to Doris. She motioned to the door lock and smiled. "Well? Do your thing."

Doris sighed and then plucked a bobby pin from her own head. With deft hands, she unlocked the door in seconds. Once inside, we were greeted with a messy room and the musty smell of unwashed laundry. There were clothes strewn all over the floor, and crumbs were everywhere. But no sign of Ian.

"That's weird. Where is he?" Doris said, checking the tiny bathroom and inside the closet.

Something about this didn't feel right. It was seven in the morning, and Ian hardly ever woke up before noon. And he wasn't the type who went out for leisurely strolls. That man was hiding something, and watching him fight with a stranger a few days ago certainly didn't help matters. "You don't think he tried to escape, do you?"

"Escape? Where could he go? We're in the middle of the Caribbean Sea. Besides, he wouldn't do that," Doris scoffed. "Unless—"

"Unless he's guilty," Monica finished for her. "We saw him with Stan. Ian must have figured out that we would put two and two together, and... now he's gone. Maybe he's hiding, so it will be easier for him to escape at the next port."

"What a nightmare," Doris mumbled. "What if it's true, and he is involved? This is Ian we're talking about. Our Ian."

"Let's not drive ourselves into a frenzy, okay? Maybe he just stepped out," said Patty Sue hopefully.

"Maybe he's in the dining room? I mean, he's always

hungry," Margie offered.

The crew dining hall was relatively empty, as well as the recreation area and the crew gym. There wasn't a peep from Ian. Before long, we found ourselves wandering by the promenade area. Some of the shops and restaurants hadn't opened yet, but the casino was already bustling with activity.

"Can I help you ladies?" called out the casino host by the door. He probably thought we were lost.

"Hi. We're looking for our friend," I said. "Around six feet tall, thin, dark hair, dresses like Maverick from *Top Gun*. Any chance you've seen him around?"

"Oh, you mean Ian?"

"Wait, you know him?" I was surprised.

"Know him? He's a regular!" he said, flashing a friendly smile. "He comes in here every day, rain or shine, stays eight hours minimum. Heck, the guys and I joke around that we should offer him a job here."

"He gambles?" Patty Sue seemed as shocked as me.

"Oh yeah. He's a regular at the poker table. A high roller if I've ever seen one."

"You know what? Maybe you're talking about a different Ian. Our Ian doesn't gamble," Doris said.

The host studied us carefully. "You ladies are The Delta Queens, right? I've seen your show. And Ian's your manager."

"That's... how did you know?" Doris stammered.

"He talks about you a lot. He talks a lot when he's gambling," he said matter-of-factly. He wasn't trying to be mean, but what he said struck a nerve.

"You know what, we just need to see him. Is he here right now?"

"That's the thing. He didn't come in today. Or yesterday

either. It's strange, actually. Is he okay?"

"We're not sure. That's why we came—"

"Stan?" I heard Monica yell, interrupting me. "Hey! Come back here!" The next thing I knew, Monica was barreling across the wooden deck, quickly followed by the rest of the girls.

What on earth?

The host looked at me in confusion. I gave him a sweet smile. "Thank you so much for your help. We'll be... right back... I think."

Then I jetted off in their direction, toward the empty lower deck, where Doris was gaining on Stan, leaving Monica in her dust. He was a big fellow, but Doris was spritely, lithe, and quick like a cheetah.

"Stop right there!"

Doris yanked him by his shirt collar and pulled him back. He crashed into a pile of empty boxes. Instead of getting back up to run, he lifted his arms as if to shield himself.

"I didn't do nothing! I swear I didn't! I'm innocent!"

Monica squatted to get eye level with him. "Will you calm down?"

"I'll tell you anything you want. Just don't hurt me!" He was starting to curl into himself. Why was he so scared? It wasn't like we were going to beat him up.

We shared a look with each other. "We're not going to hurt you, Stan. We just want to ask a few questions," Margie said.

"Oh." He looked at us like he was deciding if we were a threat or not. Then he stood up and brushed himself off. "All right then. You could have just said so."

"Really?" Monica said. "That's it? You're not going to give us a hard time?"

Stan shrugged and straightened his shirt that had become

twisted during Doris's action star takedown. Then he gestured to the pizza place that had just opened on the other side of the deck. "A little food might jog my memory. Maybe you wonderful ladies could get me a hot meal?"

* * *

"Alright, here's the deal," Stan started, his mouth half-full of pepperoni pizza. "Your precious manager's got himself a bit of a gambling problem."

We were at Sorrento's, where Stan ordered an entire pizza and a side of pasta. He was devouring the whole thing like he hadn't eaten in weeks.

Monica shook her head. "Okay, can we just start from the beginning here? How do you two know each other?"

"From the poker tables," he said. "He's a regular; I'm a regular. Gamble with a guy a few hundred times, and you know the inside of his soul, I always say."

"Ian doesn't gamble. At least, we think he doesn't," said Doris, sounding increasingly unsure by the second. The casino host knew Ian's life story, for Pete's sake. Did we even know who Ian really was?

"Oh, believe me. He does," Stan said easily. "The thing with Ian is, he gets flustered easily. Like a little kitten. When he's winning, he's got the confidence of Hercules. But when he starts to lose, he's just pfft... gone. Shaking like a leaf in the wind. And then he starts losin' and losin' and losin' and... you get my point."

He chewed while he talked until he finished the entire pizza pie. "He bought some of my products, hoping he'd turn a pretty profit. More money for him to gamble with, ya know? I mean, I don't blame him. My designer handbags are top of the line. I'm a businessman, and I trusted him. Bit of a mistake on my part." Stan started digging into the pasta, barely taking any breaths between bites. His manners flew out the window as he started talking with his mouth open, continuing his story.

"He hit that big losing streak at the casino. Threw all his money down the drain, I tell ya. Then he tried to sell my bags, so he'd have more money to throw away, ya know? And when he couldn't sell 'em, he attacked me! And out there on the deck too. For everyone to see! That was a bit of an embarrassment, I'll tell you that."

Doris leaned toward him. "Do you know where he is right now?"

"I'd be willing to bet you'll find him keeping his chair warm in the casino."

"We already checked. Ian wasn't there."

"Last time I saw him was that day captain whats-her-name laid one out on all of us. When Ian tried to beat me up, that skinny twig."

"And you haven't seen him since?" asked Monica.

"Not even a glimpse. Say, can I get another diet Coke?"

"You're pushing your luck here, Stan," Doris said as she went to grab him another drink.

I narrowed my eyes at him, taking in his greasy clothes and his unshaven appearance. Why couldn't he get his food and drinks himself? "You're not a regular passenger here, are you?"

"Nope. Smuggled myself in like a regular Isaac Gulliver," he said proudly.

"Why?"

"Because I can."

"So you're a real-life pirate!" Margie said with glee. "That's so cool." We shot Margie an incredulous look that made her squeak like a mouse when she realized what she had said.

Remembering that Monica told us Stan had a record of smuggling counterfeits, I prodded him further. "Your 'products' aren't real designer bags, are they?"

"I didn't say they were real. I just said they were top of the line," he said with a smirk.

Doris came back with a can of diet Coke and a pack of cookies. "Okay, okay. What about Carl Tanner? Do you know him?"

Stan's face lit up in recognition. "Pretty boy Carl! Oh yeah, I know him. He works for me."

"Works for you?" I questioned.

"He stores the goods for me, and he gets a small cut. Haven't heard from him in a while, though." He popped open the tab on the diet Coke and took a long sip. "Why are you asking about pretty boy Carl?"

"No reason," Margie said quickly. Stan narrowed his eyes at her but said nothing.

It looked like Margie's theories were correct. There was a smuggling operation happening on board. Both Ian and Carl were in on it.

Stan didn't need to know that Carl was now at the morgue. And Ian, meanwhile, was... out there somewhere. But where could he go? Around us, there was nothing but a bright blue ocean. Was he okay? What had he gotten himself into? Was he being held hostage somewhere? Just the thought made me sick to my stomach.

I took another look at Stan, who was now nibbling on his cookie without a care in the world. I hoped I'd never ever have to see him again.

Shocking Discovery

PATTY SUE

"Please tell me you have good news for us." Another night, another big show. The crowd on the other side of the curtain was still going wild after our encore. Any other night we would be enjoying the energy and the fame, but this time was different. Especially since our manager was still missing.

"Nothing. Not one sign of him anywhere," said Monica. She had been going around, discreetly looking for Ian. I had to admit, it was nice having someone else we could count on, especially when Captain Doherty lined up show after show for us to keep us exhausted and quiet.

Monica, however, was pumped up, bouncing on the balls of her feet and taking in everything that was going on backstage. "This is so exciting! I feel like I'm a roadie!"

"It's not very exciting when Captain Doherty is watching over us like Big Brother," said Doris with a sigh. The captain wasn't in the crowd tonight. This time, she was watching us from the upper deck of the music hall, looming over us like a mythical deity.

"This is driving me crazy." Rosemary sighed as she peeked through the curtain. The crowd was thinning, but the captain was still up there watching. "Is she spying on us right now? What's she going to do next? Have us thrown overboard? What a nerve-racking working vacation this turned out to be."

We were huddled behind the heavy curtains when Margie whispered, "Look, this all started with Carl's murder. Maybe if we solve that puzzle, then she'll lay off us."

"And what if she had something to do with *that*?" Rosemary said, shutting the curtains back together quickly as if the captain's eyes could zoom in on us.

"Then..." Doris turned to Monica. "We expose her, her smuggling operation, everything."

"What happened to laying low and not getting into trouble with the authorities?" I asked Doris.

She shook her head and smiled. "We're The Delta Queens, for Pete's sake. We're not afraid of anything."

I couldn't help but beam a smile at her. "Attagirl, Doris."

"Besides, if my daughter found out I just hid away shaking in my boots, imagine how lame she would think her ol' mom is," she said with a smirk.

"Lame? Not even for a minute! All of you ladies are a huge inspiration!" Monica cheered, still jumping on her toes.

"Well, I hate to break it to you guys, but we're right back where it happened, and we don't have a single lead," Rosemary said with a huff.

We were just a few feet away from where the lights crashed on Carl. If it weren't for all the bustling and ringing sounds backstage, I could have imagined we traveled back in time to the night of the murder.

"And why won't anyone ever answer that infernal telephone?" Margie whipped her head around, looking for the offending noise.

"The telephone," I found myself repeating. The telephone. It was ringing, loud and shrill and annoying.

Something clicked into place, and I felt myself freeze. Without thinking, my feet moved further backstage, where the ringing telephone was attached to a wall.

"Pat? Where are you going?" I heard Margie say.

A crew member picked up the ringing phone. He spoke quickly, with hurried, clipped words. When he put the phone back down, he caught me staring at him.

"Can I help you?"

"Hi, sorry. This is going to sound... weird, but was this phone ever broken?"

He looked at me like I had three heads. "This one? No. It's a new phone, just had it installed six months ago. Why would it be broken?"

"Oh, I was just wondering, that's all. Thanks."

He walked away with a slight eye roll. In a blink, everything about that night played in my mind like a vivid movie. There was Monica, chatting our ears off during our break. There was the feeling of cool water against my dry throat. And then that shrill ringing sound from backstage, cutting off Carl's voice as he called us back onstage.

The loud, sickening crash. Rick ran off to call for help. His shoes made loud squeaking noises against the floor. But then he said the phone backstage wasn't working.

"Patty Sue? Are you okay?" Doris and the rest of the girls were beside me, watching me stare at the silent phone like a weirdo.

"Rick didn't call for help that night."

"Um, yes, he did," said Rosemary. "He went to his own cabin to make the call because the phone backstage wasn't working. That's what he told me."

"Except it was working." My voice was squeaky and small. It trembled a little, but I kept going. "I just remembered. I can't believe I forgot! It was ringing and ringing when we took a break."

"Jiminy Cricket, you're right! Carl yelled at Rick to answer it," said Doris.

"Maybe something was wrong with the line at that time," countered Rosemary.

"But he didn't even go backstage to try the phone! He immediately left the music hall. Why would he even—"

A crew member materialized behind us, and we nearly jumped. He was carrying a rusty ladder and a new set of light bulbs. "Excuse me, ladies. Coming through. I just need to fix the lights over there."

"Oh right. Sorry. We'll get out of your way," said Monica.

We watched him prop the ladder and easily climb up until he reached the metal beams hanging from the ceiling. The large, heavy stage lights dangled not far from him, just within arm's reach. The same kind of lights that killed Carl.

Someone could have climbed up, walked across the catwalk, cut the cables, and caused the lights to fall. That was what I said the night after our performance when we returned to the scene of the crime to investigate.

Rick didn't call for help. And he knew the ins and outs of the backstage area better than anyone. And he was the only crew member who stayed until the end of our rehearsal. I saw Rosemary's face fall when she realized it too. Doris and Margie gasped in unison. Monica clutched her hand to her chest, looking like she was going to need that bucket again.

I stood there, wondering how I hadn't noticed it sooner. "Girls, it looks like we have one more person to investigate."

DORIS

"Hey, ladies. Wanna go get a drink?" Rick popped his head into our dressing room, his dimples already out on full display. "Everything's been packed up, and everyone's already left."

Speak of the devil. If he had popped in just a few minutes before, he might have caught wind of what we were talking about. Nevertheless, this was our chance.

"Sure thing," Rosemary said, her voice weirdly high pitched.

"Wait, really?"

"Yeah, we'd love to," I said, trying to hide the tremble from my voice. "These past few days have just been so stressful, you know?"

"Tell me about it." Rick looked taken aback that we finally accepted his offer. But he smiled again and led us out of the room. "Shall we?"

The crew bar on the lower deck was small but homey. It looked like one of those cozy dive bars we would pass by between cities while we were touring. It was all there, the neon lights, the vinyl booths and bar stools, and the sticky wood floors.

Rosemary already had a tray full of drinks before we even sat down at a booth. A pitcher of frothy beer, glasses of dark amber whiskey, and enough tequila shots to put down a horse.

"Whoa! Looks like I'm drinking in the big leagues tonight." Rick was beaming from ear to ear. Maybe this wouldn't be so hard. Let Operation Get-Rick-So-Drunk-That-He-Starts-To-Confess commence. *Okay, so we ought to have a better name for it, but our strategy is on point!*

"Drink up." Rosemary put down the tray in front of Rick and started rubbing his shoulders. "We need to loosen you up a little bit, ya know?"

"Cheers to that!" We raised a toast, and Rick gulped down his first glass of whiskey, barely even flinching from the strong, bitter taste.

"I'm surprised you guys came out tonight. I didn't think you would want to slum it with us lower folk."

"We've just been keeping a low profile. You know, after what happened with Carl," said Patty Sue, her voice dropping to a whisper.

"Oh yeah. That was terrible. A terrible, terrible thing." Rick downed another drink, this time a shot of tequila. We waited for him to say more, but he didn't. Instead, he just moved on to pour himself a beer.

"Were you and Carl close?" Monica asked, keeping her tone light and airy.

"Well, he was technically my boss."

"You've worked together before, right? On different cruise ships?"

"Yeah. Caribbean Jewel. Golden Sea Cruises. Nothing as

big as this one, though." He quickly finished his beer and then poured himself another. Then he started munching on the nuts set on the table and didn't say anything more.

"Still, all those late nights," Rosemary pushed on. "Working together backstage. You two must have gotten... close."

"I guess," he said with a sigh like he was already bored of the subject. "One time, we had this really long port call in Miami. So, he and I and a bunch of other crew guys got together at my house, fired up a barbecue, and had lunch. It was nice."

"Oh, that's right. Your wife lives in Florida!" Margie said excitedly.

"That she does," he said, his eyes turning glassy and distracted. Was he drunk already? "My beautiful wife," he mumbled.

"Okay, so about Carl..." Patty Sue tried again.

Rick started throwing back one glass after the other, not even noticing that we had barely finished our first.

"Y'know... m'wife... she loves the beach. That's why we moved to Florida."

"That's nice."

"That's why I'm working so hard, you know? So I can give her everything she wants. Everything I do, I do for her."

"Aww. That's so sweet," Margie piped in.

"We were childhood sweethearts, you know?" Rick gulped down his beer so fast I thought he just inhaled it. Why was he rambling on about his wife?

"So... umm... about Carl," I said, trying to get back on track. "Do you think Carl had any enemies?"

He ignored me and took another shot. This continued for a while, him talking about his wife and us trying to squeeze a confession out of him. Meanwhile, Rosie kept the drinks coming.

"I thought we were going to grow old together," he slurred, his voice starting to break. He was swaying slightly in his seat. Any more drinks, and he might be slumping on the table.

"Wait, what do you mean?" I asked. "Are you guys not together anymore?"

He shrugged and took another shot. His eyes were glassy and distant, like he was out of it.

"I have a picture of m'wife. Wanna see?" Before we could answer, he was fishing around for his wallet, nearly falling off his seat at the end of the booth.

"Got it!" He plopped down the wallet and showed us the photo tucked inside. "There she is, the prettiest woman in the world."

The picture was of a woman with shimmering black hair and a radiant smile posing by the beach, the golden sunlight illuminating her features. *Why do I feel like I've seen her before?*

"Oh my," Margie gasped. Rosemary's eyes bugged out of her skull. Patty Sue's jaw dropped.

Rick looked around, confused. "What?"

"Oh, nothing." Margie quickly cleared her throat and smiled. "It's just... your wife. She's pretty as a peach."

Pretty as a peach.

Oh, snap my garters! She was the woman from Carl's picture! The one we found in his desk drawer! That's why she looked so familiar. 'Wish you were here,' it said on the back. And there were the love letters. Lots and lots of cheesy love letters. 'My dearest Carl. Yours always, Natty.'

The pieces were all coming together now, falling too fast for me to catch up.

"Your wife was cheating on you with Carl," I blurted out before I could stop myself.

"Doris!" Patty Sue smacked my arm and glared at me.

"Excuse me?" In an instant, Rick's glassy eyes cleared up, replaced by something that looked like burning rage.

"So you plotted his murder. You didn't call for help that night because you wanted him dead."

My heart was racing, but I kept going. He stared me down, his boyish face contorting into something else entirely. He wasn't going to do anything to us. Not here in this crowded bar. Right?

"I don't know what you're talking about," he said easily.

"You knew the stage better than anyone. You knew where Carl was going to be, down to the second. So you climbed up to those metal beams and shredded the cables... enough that they couldn't hold the weight of the equipment."

He relaxed back in his chair and took a slow sip of his drink. "I told you, everything I do, I do for her. Carl would have crushed her like an ant under his shoe. Only I love her."

Margie's face fell to her hands. "I can't believe this. And there I was thinking about how you could never do something like this."

He set down his empty glass, his face turning blank again. "The world is a better place without people like him."

"You're going to regret saying that," said Patty Sue.

"What are you gonna do about it? You're just a bunch of old has-beens and... and talentless hacks."

"Hacks with a tape recorder," said Monica, taking out a small recorder she had hidden in her bag. "Word of advice? Don't confess to murder in the presence of a journalist."

Rick's face snapped and turned crimson. "Give me that."

"I don't think so."

"Give it to me." He hurled himself onto the table, crashing into the empty pitcher and knocking over glasses, grabbing at Monica's wrist.

"Hey! Get your hands off her!" Rosemary screeched.

Just when Rick was about to grab hold of the recorder, he got pulled away from the table like he was nothing more than a flimsy tablecloth.

"Get away from them," came a low growl.

"Ian?"

It was Ian, in his usual Maverick outfit but looking worse for wear. He looked like he hadn't showered or slept for days.

"Get your hands off me, man," Rick warned. He was still slurring and staggering, but his face was red with anger.

"Calm down, alright?"

Without warning, Rick lunged at him, throwing a wild left hook that missed Ian's face by a few inches. Ian cocked his arm, ready to answer back quickly, but before he could swing his fist, Rick fell over and slumped to the floor. His sudden loud snoring drew a few chuckles from the crowd. All the drinks Rick consumed finally worked their magic with a vengeance.

Ian looked at us like we were aliens. "You ladies mind telling me what's going on?"

"Where the heck have you been?" shrieked Rosemary. "We were worried sick!"

"What do you mean where have I been? I left you guys a note."

"What?"

Ian rolled his eyes. "You ladies really need to clean your room. I left it next to your TV."

"You didn't answer. Where have you been?"

"I was... at the brig," he muttered.

"The brig? What's that?" asked Margie.

"It's like... well, it's the jail. For the ship." He rubbed at his stubble and avoided eye contact, instead choosing to stare at Rick, still passed out on the floor.

"Why the heck would you go there?"

"It was the only way I could think of to... to keep myself away from the casino."

The casino and his gambling addiction—it was why he was acting so weird. Everything made perfect sense now. He still couldn't look at us, his face burning with shame. I put my arms around him and squeezed tight.

"Well, we're very glad that you're here. And safe."

"Very, very glad," said Rosemary. She kissed him on the head before we smooshed together into a giant group hug.

"Thanks, ladies. That means a lot. Now let's get him out of here."

"I can hardly believe it. We solved the murder mystery," said Patty Sue as we half-dragged, half-carried Rick outside. "Now what?"

I threw Ian a little wink. "Now that you're here, it looks like there's space for him in the brig."

Charting New Waters

MARGIE

"Welcome to the historic Bridgetown port of Barbados," said the cruise ship host into a microphone as throngs of passengers made their way to the gangway. "Check out the glorious beaches and the local shopping. If you pre-booked your excursion, be sure to meet your guide as you disembark. Check in at the tents just to the left. Have a great day, and remember to return to the ship before 5 pm!"

Although the gleaming emerald beaches were tempting, we decided to stay on board, making our way to the side of the crew entrance, where Carl's body was discreetly being taken away.

"What do you mean you didn't conduct an investigation?" I heard a man asking Captain Doherty. They were huddled by the entrance and so engrossed in their conversation that they didn't see us coming.

"Where's Sergeant Madeiros?" she answered. "Let me talk to him. We've known each other for years."

"He's on indefinite leave," the man said with a stern voice.

"That's preposterous. Just give him a call, and surely,

he'll—"

"Captain. Let me ask you again. Why did you not investigate this man's death?"

For the first time, I saw Captain Doherty break her composure. She fiddled with her hands and looked close to crying. "Look, maybe we can come to an agreement—"

Before she could say anything else that would get her in more hot water, like bribing this gentleman who looked like an undercover cop, I stepped in. "She did order an investigation. And she asked us to do it."

The man turned and looked at me with both eyebrows cocked. "And who are you?"

"I'm Margie. This is Doris, Patty Sue, Rosemary, and Monica. We're The Delta Queens. Well, except for Monica. She's a journalist."

He appraised us slowly. "I'm Detective Reggie Simmons."

"Well, detective, it's your lucky day. The perpetrator is already behind bars in the brig," I said confidently. Captain Doherty looked at me with her laser eyes, wondering where the heck I was going with all of this.

"What do you mean?" he asked. "What do you know about Carl's death?"

"Everything," said Doris, gesturing to the entrance of the cruise ship. "Come on inside. We have a lot to talk about."

* * *

By the time Rick was taken away for questioning, the sun had already set on the beautiful island, and the ship was preparing for departure once again. The sea was calm and dreamy, the waves crawling gently to the shore. From the corner of my eye, I spotted the captain shuffling over to us with her eyes aimed at the floor.

"I... I don't know how to thank you."

"Don't worry about it," said Patty Sue. "We just wanted to do the right thing."

"And I didn't. And I'm truly sorry for that. For everything," the captain said, her face now appearing soft and genuine.

We had figured things out with Rick, but there was one piece of the puzzle that was still missing. "Why did you want to keep things quiet? Were you afraid of losing your job if people found out?"

"I was," she said with a self-deprecating chuckle. "This isn't the first time I have had a death on my cruise ship. Ten years ago, there was a suicide. The next was just four years later, a mysterious incident that was never solved. Rick was working on that cruise, and he knew about it. I guess that's why he was so brazen. Because he knew I would want to sweep things under the rug if anything ever happened again."

"He thought he could get away with it," Rosemary said. "It was quite the trick, having you unknowingly clean up after his dirty work."

"And he would have gotten away with it too if it weren't for you all. I really shouldn't have given you such a hard time. I totally underestimated you."

"It's all water under the bridge, Captain," Monica said with a smile. "And I'm finally going to write my first crime story."

"Listen, when we get back to the states, I could talk to my brother, put in a good word for you."

"Really?" Monica squealed.

"The world needs good writers like you."

Monica squeezed the captain into a tight hug, wrinkling her

pristine white suit though she didn't seem to mind. "That's fantastic! Thank you so much!"

"And as for you lovely ladies, as long as I'm captain, there will always be a spot for you on my stage."

"Thank you, Captain," said Doris. "But I have to say, solving a murder mystery was the highlight of this cruise. I think I've been bitten by the sleuthing bug."

"Exactly! I didn't think I had it in me. Really gets the blood pumping, doesn't it?" Rosemary said, her face bright and excited.

Patty Sue nodded. "I mean, don't get me wrong, making music and performing will always be magical for me, but this... this is something else entirely. Feels like we made a real difference."

"And when we pieced the puzzle together and figured out about Carl's affair? I felt like Sherlock Holmes!" I squealed.

The ladies and I looked at each other, communicating in that special way we always had. Maybe we were older. Maybe we didn't sell records like we used to. Maybe we were a bunch of older has-beens. But we had a great run at our musical dream, and somehow, I knew we were ready to let go and move on to other things. It was time. My face broke into a grin, thrilled about the prospect. "Maybe it's time for something new? Something like... a crime squad."

"Yes! Like private detectives!" Rosemary exclaimed. "This could be the end of one chapter of our lives and the beginning of another."

"Are you sure?" Captain Doherty said. "It's a little scary, starting something new, isn't it?"

"A little," Doris answered. She flashed a smile as we hooked our arms together and looked out over the calm sea.

MURDER AT HIGH SEA

"But at least we have each other," I added. "It may not always be smooth sailing... but together, I know we'll find our way."

THE END

If you enjoyed meeting the Delta Queens and like twisty mysteries that take place in the south, I've got something very special in store for you in the second Piper Sandstone series!

When an art heist ends in murder, can Piper and her senior crime-fighting gal pals catch the killer before she gets marked off their hit list?

Find out in the next thrilling, hilarious, and heartwarming mystery adventure.

Snag your copy of *Bacon, Bodyguards, and Ballistics* with the QR code below and dive into the next deliciously thrilling whodunit!

She's a Chicago detective hiding in a seaside town with a lot to prove...and everything to lose.

Don't miss the next hilarious and thrilling Piper Sandstone adventure in Savory, Alabama!

Snag your copy of *Bacon, Bodyguards, and Ballistics* with the QR code below and get ready to devour a deep fried revenge murder mystery!

Sneak Peek

Bacon, Bodyguards, and Ballistics
From the Prologue

It was a bright winter day in Savory, Alabama, but in Mayor Alice Townsend's office, a heavy, gray cloud loomed above us. She was gnawing at her nails and pacing back and forth until her chunky heels left imprints on the blue carpet.

"We are in the middle of a PR nightmare in this town," Mayor Townsend stated the obvious as she shook her finger high above her head. "Savory, Alabama is supposed to be a cozy town. Quiet. Safe. The kind of sleepy little coastal place you want to bring your family to for vacation." I looked her straight in the eyes and nodded quietly in agreement.

"You know what it's NOT?" Her bright green eyes were wide and manic, hands flip-flopping in the air. "A hotspot for murders and serial killers!"

I stood rooted to the spot in front of her desk. Beside me was Jake, the tough-guy sheriff of the aforementioned cozy little town. It felt like high school again, and we were taking a tongue-lashing in the principal's office. Only Alice was much prettier to look at, even with her anxious nail-biting and huffing.

Being the bearer of bad news was never fun or easy, but somebody had to do it, and today that somebody happened to be us.

"I mean, didn't we have enough last summer?" she said, falling to her chair with a tired groan. "Poor Marco Jenkins. I've known his family since they were kids."

Marco Jenkins. The subject of said bad news. Early twenties. Savory born and raised. Worked as a security guard on one of the estates near town. A quiet kid, from what I'd heard. Kept his head down and his nose clean.

So, it was quite the shock when a poor mailman found his body floating in Cold Stone Creek. With a knife firmly lodged in his back.

"An investigation is underway, Mayor," Jake piped up. "I assure you, we'll be—"

"Jake, the Queen Bee's Private Eyes will be working with the sheriff's department to solve this case," the mayor said before turning her head to me. "That's why I called you here today, Sharon."

"What? You can't be serious, Mayor!"

"Hey!"

"No offense, but it's far too dangerous. We don't really know what we're dealing with here."

"Exactly," the mayor said without missing a beat. "We need all the help we can get. And the Delta Queens—and Sharon, too, of course—certainly stepped up last summer."

I gave her a proud, wide grin but then toned it down when I remembered we were dealing with a murder. Again.

"Fine," Jake resigned. "But you better do exactly as we say."

"I make no promises," I said with a smirk. He bristled slightly but then shook his head with a faint smile.

"We need to know all the details," I said, taking out my notepad and getting straight to business. "Who was he last with?"

Jake's blue eyes turned icy, his face sour like he just remembered something terrible. "CCTV footage showed him leaving a bar with his twin brother."

"His twin?" Mayor Alice stopped gnawing at her nails as her big eyes widened even further. "You mean Max?"

Jake's nod was grim.

"Yes, Max. And we have reason to believe that he murdered his brother."

* * *

Snag your copy of *Bacon, Bodyguards, and Ballistics* with the QR code below, and get ready to devour a deliciously fun and thrilling cozy mystery that is unputdownable! Mouthwatering recipes included!

Would you like more Delta Queen mystery adventures?

P.S. Thank you for reading Murder at High Sea. I hope you enjoyed getting to meet the Delta Queens as they discover their newfound passion for sleuthing. Would you like to see more of the Delta Queen's mystery adventures?

If so, I'd like to ask for a small favor. Would you be so kind as to leave a review on Amazon? Writing is my passion, and I look forward to *your* feedback. Your honest opinion helps me create my best work for you.

Thank you!

Karen

Scan Barcode to Leave a Review:

FREE GIFT

Receive your FREE exclusive copy of **Hash Browns And Homicide**, the series prequel, and get notified via email of new releases, giveaways, contests, cover reveals, and insider fun when you sign up to my VIP Mystery Book Club mailing list!

Karen McSpade

Hash Browns And Homicide

A Piper Sandstone Savory Mystery

Scan the QR Code To Sign Up and Claim Your FREE Exclusive Book

Books By Karen McSpade

The Savory Mystery Series

Hash Browns And Homicide

Murder and Grits

Red Beans And R.I.P.

Mystery On the Half Shell

Killer Gumbo

Crab Cake Criminal

Murder at High Sea

The Deep Fried Revenge Series

Pies & Pilfering (Prequel)

Bacon, Bodyguards, and Ballistics - Book 1

Bacon, Bodyguards, and Ballistics - Book 2

Bacon, Bodyguards, and Ballistics - Book 3

Bacon, Bodyguards, and Ballistics - Book 4

Bacon, Bodyguards, and Ballistics - Book 5

Crystal Beach Magic Mystery Series

Cat Scratch Murder

Claw of Attraction

Feline Like a Suspect

A Meowing Suspicion

Paws in Space

Witch Under Pressure

Witch in the Middle

A Grave Mistake

Tangled in Magic

Charmed and Dangerous

Holiday Cozy Mysteries & Mystery Romance

Christmas Cakes and Crooks

Scan QR Code to visit Karen McSpade's Books online

About the Author

Raised in the Arkansas River Valley, Karen McSpade grew up with a fishing pole in one hand and her trusty .410 shotgun in the other. Exploring the creeks and woods around her hometown while hunting with her father kept her "entertained and out of jail," as her mom likes to say.

As a child, her most prized possessions were her books and her Michael Jackson album collection. These led her to a brief venture into breakdancing and poetry slamming before discovering her true passion, bringing stories and characters to life. Today, she focuses on the two things that still inspire her creativity—her love for food and dishing up mysteries with a dash of humor.

Karen's novels feature compassionate and strong-willed leading ladies determined to uncover the truth and seek justice. She loves creating stories filled with mystery, romance, magic, and adventure that allow readers to join her characters on their journey, leaving behind the real world for a few hours at a time.

When she's not writing, Karen's favorite things are spending time with family, traveling, cooking, reading, gardening, and enjoying nature. She lives in Northwest Arkansas with her family and a very spoiled Wheaten Terrier who doubles as her writing assistant.

Join Karen on Facebook for updates, fun, and prizes!

Made in the USA
Monee, IL
13 March 2024

54847161R00075